Also by Anne White:  **W9-BDW-877**

An Affinity For Murder

BENEATH THE SURFACE

Anne White

Anne White

October 23, 2005

HILLIARD HARRIS

Clifton Park - Halfmoon Public Library
475 Moe Road
Clifton Park, New York 12065

P.O. Box 3358
Frederick, Maryland 21705-3358

First Edition-June 2005
ISBN 1-59133-124-2

9588

Book Design: S. A. Reilly
Cover Illustration © S. A. Reilly
Manufactured/Printed in the United States of America
2005

ACKNOWLEDGMENTS

My sincere thanks to:

Stephanie and Shawn E. Reilly of Hilliard and Harris for accepting and publishing my manuscript.

Grace Morgan for her encouragement and suggestions.

The Malice Domestic organization for awarding me an Unpublished Writers' Grant in 1999 and a Best First Mystery nomination in 2002.

Matt Witten, television script writer, producer and author of the Jacob Burns mystery series set in nearby Saratoga Springs, NY for being a super teacher and adviser.

Rick Morin of Morin's Dive Center of Glens Falls for sharing the secrets of raising articles of all kinds from *beneath the surface.*

John Strong and the Lake George Arts Project for their outstanding writing workshops.

The Unusual Suspects Mystery Writers for their helpful critiques and suggestions.

And a special thank you to:

My son, Michael White, Executive Director of the Lake George Park Commission, for sharing his knowledge of the lake and its artifacts.

And my daughter, Kate White, magazine editor and author of the Bailey Weggins mystery series, for a hundred and one helpful tips on writing, editing and publishing

CHAPTER ONE

I'M GIVING EMERALD Point six months," I told friends in Manhattan the day I took my grandfather's house off the market and moved into it.

Four years later I was still there.

In that time I'd cobbled together a new life. Step by step, I renovated the rambling old Victorian I'd loved since childhood, tempered my city-style political activism to an acceptable small-town level and--in a move even more astounding to me than to the local politicos--got myself elected mayor of our village.

Although I suffered occasional misgivings, I refused to second guess myself. For the most part I was satisfied, comfortable with my decision and with my place in the world. And that place, for the time being at least, was a corner of upstate New York, two hundred fifty miles north of the city and light years away from everything I'd once considered important.

"I've thought of a new spot for your run," my sixteen-year-old friend Josie Donohue informed me one day when I stopped at her mother's restaurant. Josie scorned outdoor activities herself, but she knew everything there was to know about the Point and its environs. "Drive up 9N and turn off on--let's see--the third right after Beacon Hill Drive. Just your ticket--a dirt road along the lake."

For a confirmed couch potato, the girl had good instincts. The next morning a little before seven, I followed her directions, allowed a few extra minutes for warm-up stretches and took off along the rutted path she'd suggested. The June sun burned hot on my back, but the air was fresh and cool, without the humidity, which would make running such a drag later in the summer. As always, the beauty of Lake George dazzled me--thirty-two miles of slate-blue water, surrounded by low green hills, under a cloudless sky.

I'd covered about half a mile when I caught sight of a boy hunkered down in the grass ahead of me. I didn't recognize him, but that didn't surprise me. I still didn't know all the local kids by name. This one looked to be somewhere in his teens--shaggy black hair, jeans wet and crusted with dirt. He watched me approach with the dazed expression of an accident victim.

"What happened?" I glanced toward the water fifteen feet below at the foot of a steep bank. I assumed he'd tumbled in somehow and climbed back up.

"Bike." He pointed at a bike, more accurately a bike minus its front wheel, lying a few feet away.

"You fell over that?" I shuddered, picturing him tripping on the unexpected obstacle and taking a nosedive down the rocky incline.

"No. Goddamn it. I was riding it."

"But how did you get wet?"

The boy shook his head, sending droplets of water flying around him. He brushed at the muddy dirt on his scraped hands, then slid them carefully along his pants legs. He winced as he touched his knees.

I waited, hoping for a better explanation of what had happened to him.

"Wheel came off," he muttered finally.

He got up with difficulty and limped to the edge of the cliff. I hung in close behind him. He pointed down the slope to where a bike wheel was caught on an outcropping of rock just above the water line. "Damn thing rolled there."

He looked much too shaky to go after the wheel himself, so I sat down and began sliding on my butt from rock to rock. I'd reached the midpoint of the embankment when I realized the boy was trailing along behind me. Despite the steepness of the descent, he kept one arm wrapped around his waist as if something hurt him.

"Wait. Look over there." He pointed toward a spot in the lake a few yards off shore.

At first, I couldn't see anything but water. Then I focused on a dark red mass just below the surface. My breath caught in my throat as I realized I wasn't looking at a rock or a submerged tree. "That's a car down there. Do you think somebody could be in it?"

"Thought maybe. I swam out." He stared past me at the lake.

"Well, is there?"

He shook his head. "See that wavy shadow? Driver's side? I thought that was somebody sitting there, but it isn't. The car's empty."

"How could a car be down there? This path's too narrow to drive on."

"Could, if you were careful. Maybe somebody wanted to get rid of the car. The windows are all open."

I felt a cold chill, a sense that I was hurtling pell-mell toward something I didn't want to confront. Emerald Point didn't have its own police force but, as mayor, I was kept informed about the investigations the county sheriff's department handled in the village. I had a bad feeling about this car.

"Could you tell the make?" I asked.

"It's a dark red four-door. A Chevy." The boy inched his way back up the bank, still holding one arm across his midsection.

I pulled my cell phone out of the pocket of my sweat pants and handed it up to him. I made an effort to keep my voice steady. "We'll have to let the sheriff's department know. Take this and call 911. Tell 'em the mayor's reporting a car in the lake."

"You the mayor?" He sucked in his lower lip as he considered whether or not to believe me.

"That's right. Loren Graham. What's your name?"

"Todd. Todd Lewis."

"Well, Todd, tell 'em to send the rescue squad, too. Your bike's wrecked and I don't think you should try to walk. You could have internal injuries."

"I'm all right. I don't want no rescue squad guys pokin' at me."

"Why don't you let me take a look, see how banged up you really are. Maybe we shouldn't be wasting time here," I said.

He clutched his wet tee shirt more tightly around him. "I looked. Just bruised a little. Don't make a big deal of it." He scuttled one-handed over the top of the bank and out of sight.

I eased my body down the slope. Belatedly, I considered the possibility that the boy would take off with my cell phone and disappear. I'd certainly lost most of the survival skills I'd honed during my years in New York.

With my eyes fixed on the wheel, I slid along until I was close enough to reach for it. After two or three tries I got a good grip on the rim and yanked. The wheel came loose with a force that nearly knocked me off balance. I steadied myself, then inched backward up the slope, moving toward my left where I spotted what looked like an easier way to climb to the top. Still hanging onto the wheel, I sidled along until I reached a section of rocks where I could turn around and pull myself up.

I'd managed only a short distance when I saw something that stopped me cold--first, sneaks, soggy, decomposing sneaks poking out from under a scraggly bush; then, half buried by leaves and dirt, rotted jeans with something mushy underneath that might have once been legs. Even worse, I smelled the awful, sickening odor of decaying flesh. I was smelling death and I knew it. I flung both hands across my nose and mouth, fighting back nausea.

"Hey. Bring the phone this way," I gasped.

I heard the boy shuffling along the bank above me. In less than a minute he peered over the edge.

"What the hell?"

"Don't try to come down. I've found a body. Call 911 again. Tell 'em to get here fast." I turned away and vomited my morning coffee over the rocks, retching time and time again, unable to stop.

The boy started down the embankment. "Hang on. I'm coming. Are you sure it's a body?"

"Call 911. Call right away." I forced the words out between spasms of dry heaves

I couldn't say anything more. Even after I calmed down and started to creep back up the embankment, I couldn't speak. I concentrated on taking slow, deep breaths. My insides settled a little, but the shakiness spread outward to my arms and legs. I hung onto a rock, trembling, afraid if I loosened my grip I'd topple head first down the slope into the water. A sick feeling built and crashed and rebuilt inside me, breaking like the white-caps pounding against the rocks below. I knew what I'd found. As much as I didn't want to believe it, I knew exactly what I'd found.

CHAPTER TWO

BY THE TIME I reached the top of the bank, Todd Lewis had used my cell phone to summon help. I sank down on a rock near him still feeling waves of nausea wash over me. Sweat matted my hair and soaked through my tee shirt and running shorts.

Sheriff's Deputy Rick Cronin arrived within fifteen minutes of Todd's call. He sped down the narrow dirt road as if it were a multi-lane highway. He slammed his white patrol car to a stop in front of us. With a quick turn of the wheel, he pulled onto the grass, leaving space for the other vehicles we could hear approaching.

As Rick jumped out of his car and hurried toward us, I felt a surge of relief. At twenty-five, Rick was the youngest man on the county force, but in his dark gray uniform and broad-brimmed gray hat he looked capable of handling any emergency.

"You okay, Mayor? You, Todd? Rescue squad's coming right along."

In his slow, methodical style, Rick took Todd step by step through his bicycle accident and the discovery of the car in the lake. Then he turned his attention to me.

"Take your time, Mayor. Tell me exactly how you found the body," he said.

I took a deep breath and told him how I'd climbed down after Todd's wheel and how he'd followed me to point out the car in the lake. When I got to the part where I'd seen the body, I felt my stomach churn as if I were going to be sick all over again.

As soon as the ambulance arrived, Rick turned us over to one of the EMTs and scooted down the bank. To my relief, he didn't ask me to go along to point out the location of the remains. I'd seen all I wanted to see of that decomposing corpse. At some point I knew someone would say the name, Tammy Stevenson, but I hoped I didn't have to be the one to do it.

5

Once I'd convinced the EMT I didn't need medical help, he turned his attention to Todd. He needed all his persuasive powers to talk Todd into lifting his shirt and showing him the ugly scrape that ran diagonally across his chest and stomach. He studied it seriously for several minutes and pronounced it "painful but not serious." After getting Todd's reluctant okay, he applied a soothing ointment to the scrape and to the other bruises he noticed. He then followed Rick down the slope to inspect the body.

Ten minutes later I was still huddled on the rock when Warren County Sheriff's Investigator Jim Thompson drove up. Jim didn't wear the department uniform, but even in his navy blazer and slacks, he projected a look of command.

He'd brought along the county coroner, Dr. Stuart Tarryton. He was a genial guy, trim and white-haired, well into his sixties and in super shape. Doc nodded in my direction, then vaulted over the top of the embankment and disappeared from view.

"You two sit tight. I'll be back in a few minutes to take your statements." Jim rolled his eyes at me and followed Doc over the bank.

He returned a short time later and squatted down next me. "Would have been embarrassing if I broke my leg leaping around after a guy with twenty years on me. I'd say that was Tammy Stevenson's body down there. Looks like she didn't make it out of town after all."

So there it was--the report I'd expected to hear. The disappearance over a year before of Tammy Stevenson, a local high school student, had shocked everyone in Emerald Point and set tongues wagging all around the lake. Gossip circulated that the beautiful, precocious seventeen year old had run off, possibly with an out-of-town boyfriend. A few people, especially her mother Melissa Taggert, insisted she'd come to harm.

That morning I asked Jim the question I knew would be repeated dozens of times that day. "How in the world could she have ended up down there? Do you think she went in with the car, then climbed part way up the bank before she collapsed?"

"Possible," Jim said.

"Does it look like that's what happened?" I persisted.

"Don't know. That's what we have to determine."

I shuddered. Of all the things I'd thought might have happened to Tammy Stevenson, I hadn't pictured her injured, unable to summon help, dying all alone in a remote spot like this. I found myself hoping we were wrong, that the body would turn out to be someone else. Still, no matter who was lying down there on the embankment, this lonely death wasn't a fate I'd wish on anyone.

CHAPTER THREE

THE NEXT HOUR dragged mercilessly. Jim questioned Todd and me together, then separately, pushing us to remember details we'd overlooked the first time we'd told our stories. When he finally accepted the fact we weren't going to come up with anything more, he granted reluctant permission for us to leave. Rick Cronin loaded Todd's bike and wheel into his trunk, then drove me to my car and took off to give Todd a ride home.

By the time I'd grabbed a shower and headed for the office it was after eleven o'clock. I unlocked the front door of the white A-frame known as the Village Building--we'd never use a name as grand as Town Hall here in Emerald Point--and belatedly started my daily ritual. Computer turned on, blinds open, coffee maker dripping my favorite brand.

As soon as I could squeeze out enough coffee for a cup, I filled my mug and collapsed in the chair behind my desk. I pulled my in-box toward me, but I couldn't focus on the papers spilling out of it. I couldn't think about anything except Tammy Stevenson.

My brain cells scurried around, scarfing up bits of information I'd read or heard, piecing the story together. Tammy Stevenson—different last name from her mother--thought to be a runaway, but no one had ever figured out where she'd run to. The sheriff's department had investigated and found no evidence she'd been the victim of foul play. Jim Thompson, who took responsibility for most of the cases the sheriff's department handled in this part of the county, had kept me informed. On a spring night more than a year ago, Tammy had quarreled with her mother and stormed out of the house. No one had reported seeing her since.

I was still slouched over my desk, staring at the stack of papers when Pauline Collins burst through the front door.

"Are you all right, Loren? I didn't know if you'd be here or not. I figured I better get in and cover the office in case you were tied up all day."

As always, news had traveled fast in Emerald Point. Pauline, the conscientious secretary, had heard about my role in the discovery of Tammy Stevenson's body and was jumping in to help.

The position of mayor of our little community wasn't considered a full-time job, but I thought someone should be in the office for as much of the day as possible. To do that, I'd worked out a schedule with Pauline which satisfied us both. I covered the office in the mornings; she came in afternoons.

As with so much else in Emerald Point, Pauline couldn't be pigeonholed easily. White-haired, short and plump, she looked like one of those bustling, grandmotherly types who brought their special casseroles to church suppers or displayed exquisite handiwork at craft fairs. She'd served for many years as secretary to our former mayor, affectionately known even in his seventies as Young Ned Chamberlain. She knew all the village secrets, not just those from her own lifetime, but from generations before. Prying them out of her wasn't always easy, but I was getting better at it all the time.

After my election the preceding fall, I'd listed the problems I might face as mayor, ranking them in order of importance. Once Young Ned had announced he was retiring to Florida, I moved Pauline's name in block letters to the top of my list. She'd idolized the gregarious, outgoing Ned and I questioned how she'd adapt to working with someone new. And not just new, but more than three decades younger than Ned and woefully inexperienced.

Within a week of my swearing in on New Year's Day, I was giving thanks for Pauline's keen mind, her insights into local affairs and the discretion which enabled her to keep sensitive information to herself. If she found me a poor substitute for her former boss, she possessed enough tact not to let on.

The morning I found Tammy Stevenson's body, I bided my time until Pauline had her computer humming and her desk arranged to her liking. Asking Pauline questions before she'd sorted through her in-box was more futile than talking to me before I'd finished my morning coffee.

When she looked ready to face the day, I said, "Pauline, tell me what you remember about Tammy Stevenson's disappearance."

"Well, I remember Melissa bugged Ned about it until he was half out of his mind, but you couldn't help but feel sorry for her.

Thought sure something terrible had happened to Tammy and the sheriff's department wasn't taking her disappearance seriously. Now, looks like she was right."

"I remember a lot of gossip at the time she disappeared. People thought she'd run off with somebody," I said.

"They couldn't come up with a name, though. Tammy had quite the reputation for a young girl, but nobody pointed the finger at anyone in particular. Another story making the rounds was that she couldn't get on with the stepfather."

"And that's Bob Taggert, right? What kind of a guy is he?"

"Bob Taggert? No different from a lot of men. Hard worker, decent enough guy sober, obnoxious drunk. Fortunately, he keeps his nose clean most of the time. All those Taggerts tended to be mean drunks. The old man was the worst."

"Has the family lived around here for a long time?"

"Three, maybe four generations, I'd say. Kin to the Reynolds, you know. And the Bronsons."

"Really," I said. Sometimes it seemed as if everyone in Emerald Point was related. It was a standing joke among newcomers in town that we should never dis' anybody since we were probably talking to the person's relatives.

"I used to be in the rescue squad with Bob and Melissa, the fire company, too. Good workers, both of 'em. Decent folk. Not as smooth talkin' as some, but they don't pretend to be something they're not." High praise coming from Pauline.

People like the Taggerts formed the backbone of Emerald Point and its organizations. Descendants of the farmers and lumberjacks who settled the region, many of them commuted to blue collar jobs in nearby mills or to stores and offices in Glens Falls and Queensbury. Sometimes, when the Point's upper echelon--the wealthy businessmen and summer residents who owned the elegant lakeside homes--threw their weight around, I'd ask Pauline to fill me in on the middle-class families who were also my constituents, even if they were much less vocal about it.

"Tell me again about the Taggerts. They have other children besides Tammy, don't they?"

Consulting Pauline on a family history was like giving a cat a saucer of cream. I could almost see her licking her lips as she settled back in her chair.

"Well, the Taggerts are one of those 'his, hers and theirs' families. Bob has a son, Rob, somewhere in his mid-twenties. Tammy is Melissa's daughter by her first husband."

"Was he from here, too?" I asked.

"Came from over in New England somewhere. Left Melissa high and dry after she had that baby. Took off and, as I hear tell, never sent her a penny in child support. Melissa didn't have an easy time of it before she hooked up with Bob Taggert."

"And Bob had a child himself?"

Pauline nodded. "That's right. Then they had a couple more kids together."

"That couldn't have been easy. Think there was some sibling rivalry?"

"How could there help but be? As I understand it, Tammy was always a handful. The last few years she really ran wild. Melissa had a time with her from what I hear tell. She was flunkin' school, getting into bars with a fake ID, then expected Melissa to throw her a big seventeenth birthday party. That's what the fight was about, I guess."

"I wish I could place this girl. I've probably seen her, but I don't remember what she looked like."

"Oh, you'd remember if you'd seen her up close. She was a beautiful girl. Looked more like a movie star than your average teenager. Drove around town in a big red clunker of a car. Melissa let her have that car. I don't understand why parents do things like that."

"You're talking about the car they found in the lake?"

"I suppose that's it. The sheriff put out one of those all-points bulletins about it, but nobody ever reported seeing it. Of course, people said she could have junked it. It was that old and beat up."

But she hadn't junked it. Somehow the car had disappeared into the lake and Tammy Stevenson, the high-spirited girl with the movie star looks, had died a lonely death on a bank nearby.

CHAPTER FOUR

THE NEWS OF the discovery of a body swept through our little town. The coroner, using dental records from a Glens Falls dentist, made the identification quickly and his findings confirmed the suspicions already circulating as truth. Definitely Tammy Stevenson's remains. Determining the cause of death would take more time.

The next morning, Jim arrived at my office in the Village Building at exactly eight-fifteen--a sure sign he had something on his mind. He pushed the door shut behind him and pulled up a chair across from me.

"Todd Lewis. What was his demeanor yesterday when you came on him?"

Demeanor? When Jim used words as formal as that, he meant business. I kept my answer short and serious.

"Dazed, hurting. I thought he'd banged himself up pretty bad the way he was hunched over, holding onto himself."

"Suspicious acting, maybe? Would you say he seemed to know more than he was telling?"

"Jim, come on. Do you know any teenagers who don't fit that description?"

He made a non-committal grunt.

I thought carefully about what he'd asked me.

"But, no, I didn't see it that way. Tammy had been dead a long time. You can't be thinking he had something to do with her death," I said.

"Not then, of course. But maybe he knew the body was there."

"That doesn't make sense, Jim. He was sitting by the path, but he couldn't have known someone would turn up. And the wheel had come off his bike. We all saw that."

"Then there's the fact that he was wet."

"He said he swam out to check the car. Do you think he was lying about that?" I asked.

"What I'm doing here is trying to determine if everything was the way he said it was or not. When you told him you'd found a body, did he seem surprised? I'm wondering if he knew the body was there before that."

"No way," I started to say, but I caught myself. I'd attributed Todd's dazed state to his fall from the bike, but my assumption could have been way off base.

"We'll check him out, of course. See if there's anything to tie him to Tammy's disappearance. They were in the same class at the high school, knew each other pretty well, I guess. But from what we're hearing, Tammy didn't bother much with kids her own age."

"You've talked to her mother, of course."

"Not much help there right now. She's ticked off at all of us. We're going to get the car out this afternoon. Maybe that will give us some leads."

"You're going to raise the car? Can I be there?"

"Don't see why not. We've got a dive team coming to take charge of the operation. Two o'clock if you want to see how it's done."

I did, and I didn't.

AT ONE-THIRTY I steeled myself and went back to the site. I added my car to several others in the nearest parking area and walked back along the narrow dirt road. A group of men, most of them local, had gathered on the bank. Jim and Rick Cronin stood apart, staring down at the water. I walked over to them.

"I wanted to see how they do this," I told Jim. "I know all kinds of vehicles go into the lake for one reason or another, but I guess I've never thought much about how they're taken out."

Jim nodded in my direction. "You'll find out right now. These guys are experts from a dive shop in Glens Falls. They're using something called a VRS-2000. That's a self-contained vehicle recovery system. Watch how they do it. It's quite an operation."

A diver stripped to his trunks and slipped into the water. As we watched, he dove down to attach a flotation bag to the front bumper of the car. As soon as it was secured, he swam around and fastened another bag to the rear bumper.

"Don't they have to put something under the car to raise it?" I asked.

"Sometimes they do," Jim said, "but this is a pretty simple operation. They rig the bags to cradle the vehicle. They could connect the chains together and pass 'em underneath it if they needed to. This time, it doesn't look as if they'll have to do that."

The diver paddled away from the car and the bags began to inflate.

Jim stepped closer to the edge of the cliff and peered down. "I've watched these guys do this before and they've explained the process to me. They use two-thousand pound flotation bags and an aluminum scuba cylinder. The cylinder fills the bags and, barring unforeseen problems, that car's gonna pop right to the surface in a matter of minutes."

He was right. As I watched in amazement, the car rose from the bottom of the lake and appeared to float on the water.

"You mean that's it?" I asked in surprise.

Matt Tremont, our local douser, detached himself from the group of men on the bank and walked over to us.

"Did they call you for this one?" Jim asked him.

"Just thought I'd stop by. Don't guess they're going to need me for anything."

"Matt, do you help out with things like this?" I said.

"Somebody suggested I be here. Thought they might need dousing done in the cove, but they've already finished their search. They wondered if they might find other bodies or something suspicious near the car, but I guess they didn't turn up anything. So I'll go along." He moved off down the path toward the parking area.

"Nothing to douse for on this one," Rick Cronin said. "And no body to get out of the car--that would make the job harder. The water's warm now, too. They don't have to contend with ice the way they do sometimes in winter."

"But how are they going to get the car up the cliff?" I asked

"They'll float it along until they reach a level place where they can bring it out," Jim said. "This won't be like the rescue I saw one time where they had to pull a snowmobile a long way under the ice before they could raise it This car may be pretty banged up, but they should be able to get it up on shore without much trouble."

Jim's predictions proved accurate. The operation went smoothly since the dive team apparently knew exactly what to do and how to do it. The crowd, satisfied they'd seen what they came for, began to disperse. Tom Bailey and Peter Finch, local motel owners, tossed us a friendly wave as we walked toward our cars.

Things were moving fast, I thought, as I drove back to the office. Tammy's body had been identified and her car pulled from the lake. A few days at the most, and the sheriff's department would have wrapped up the case.

I couldn't have been more wrong.

CHAPTER FIVE

THE NEXT AFTERNOON when Pauline came in to work, I ran an idea by her.

"I thought I might stop by the Taggerts' and express my sympathy. I hear they're not having a wake, just a private burial once the coroner releases the body," I said.

Pauline agreed at once. "That would be a very nice thing to do, Loren. I'm sure Melissa would appreciate it."

I'd never seen being mayor of Emerald Point as such a big deal, but one of the many things I'd learned since January was that other people often did. I wolfed down a quick lunch and took off.

The Taggerts lived in a neighborhood of small ranch houses on the northwest outskirts of Emerald Point. The houses in their development had been considered a terrific investment when they went on the market a dozen years before. By this time, many of them needed paint and repairs, but I didn't minimize the importance of the development. The availability of housing like this meant the world to middle-income families like the Taggerts. One of my first acts in office had been to apply for a Small Cities Grant to make money available to these owners for renovations.

I'd rung the bell twice before Melissa opened the front door. I didn't expect to find her dressed in black and rending her garments, but her appearance gave me a jolt. In her neat white slacks and freshly-ironed pink cotton shirt, she looked slimmer and more girlish than I remembered, nowhere near old enough to have a child Tammy's age. She was carrying a bottle of window cleaner and a roll of paper towels, but her hair and makeup were more suited to an evening out than an afternoon of housework.

"Mayor, what are you doing here?" she asked. Not quite the reaction Pauline had predicted.

"I wanted to say how sorry I am about Tammy. I guess I've caught you at a bad time."

She hesitated. "No, no. It's all right. I'm expecting two of Bob's sisters tomorrow. They were both real nice to Tammy, treated her just like she was his. I wanted the house clean for them. Come in."

It was my turn to hesitate.

"I can stop by another time."

"No. You're here now. You might as well come in. I'm done with the living room. Let's sit in there." She led me to the couch and sat down in a chair opposite me. The scent of lemon furniture polish mingled with Melissa's cologne. The dark wood of the coffee table gleamed in a shaft of sunlight.

Melissa glanced anxiously toward the kitchen. I heard the scrape of a chair being moved and footsteps on the tiled floor. I looked up, expecting to see Bob Taggert.

Instead, it was Tom Bailey who came through the kitchen door. Tanned and muscular, wearing khaki shorts and white tennis shirt, Tom looked more like a summer tourist than a local motel owner.

Melissa glared at him as she stumbled through a half-hearted introduction. "You two know each other, don't you?"

Tom gave a quick nod in my direction. "I'll stop back when Bob's here, Mel. Help him move that stuff out of the garage before your in-laws get here." He whirled around and disappeared into the kitchen. We heard the slam of the back door.

Melissa, painfully ill at ease, felt the need to explain his presence. "Tom's supposed to help with something, but Bob went to work today. He can't keep taking time off. We don't know yet when the funeral's going to be."

Her embarrassment made me uncomfortable, too.

"So you really can't make plans," I offered.

"That's right. They have to do an autopsy. They told us we've got to wait for that," Melissa said.

"And they can't give you any idea when it'll be completed?"

She shook her head. "No, they're taking their time with it."

The conversation ground to a halt.

Finally, Melissa leaned forward in her chair and looked directly at me for the first time.

"I have to know. They told me you're the one who found her. Had she been hurt real bad?"

I wanted to say something reassuring, but I couldn't find the words. "I really didn't see much, her sneaks mostly."

"That's all?"

"I knew I'd found a body and I thought it might be Tammy because I'd already seen the red car in the water."

"Did you see her shoulder bag near her any place? She always had that bag with her."

"A pocketbook, you mean?"

"A *Coach* bag, tan colored, real nice leather, even had her monogram on it."

"No. I didn't see anything like that. But maybe they found it when they searched the area."

"If they did, they haven't told me about it. Tammy had high falutin' ideas. She bought that pocketbook over in Manchester at the *Coach* outlet. Real pricey, but nothing would do 'til she got one. Then she carried it everywhere, about went crazy if any of the rest of us touched it."

"Are you thinking she might have been robbed?"

Her face twisted with grief. "Robbed? I don't know. Somebody killed her, but I don't even know why they did it—or where. Somebody killed her and dumped her body."

That wasn't what I expected to hear. "But the car was in the lake. I thought maybe there'd been an accident and she'd managed to get out of the car somehow."

"I thought that, too, at first. I drove out to the place she was found. The sheriff's department had that yellow tape strung all around and a guard sitting there. He said they'd already seen people snoopin' around and wanted the area secured until they finished searching it."

"Had you told them about the pocketbook? Was that what they were searching for?"

"I mentioned it, I guess. That Thompson asked me a bunch of questions and told me diddly in return. All I've found out is that the injury in her skull didn't come from any accident. More like somebody hit her with something."

"And the investigator told you this?"

"God, no. Didn't I just say he won't tell me anything? A friend of mine who works in the hospital found out from the woman who types up the coroner's notes."

I believed her. This was exactly the way things happened around here.

Her eyes filled with tears and she wiped them away.

"There's all kinds of stories making the rounds. People are havin' a field day, gossiping about us. Now they're spreading it all around town that Tammy was murdered. And I had to hear it third hand."

"Melissa, I'm sorry. I wish there was some way I could help." I reached across the space between us and touched her hand.

"I'll tell you what you can do. They're going to shove this on the back burner, I know they are. They'll let it drop, just like they've done all year. Tammy didn't have a good reputation around town, and I'm not important. If Bob and I owned a big place on the lake, they'd be jumping through hoops for us. You know what I hear people are saying? They're saying Tammy got what she was asking for. She was seventeen years old. She had her whole life ahead of her, and this was what she was asking for?" She covered her face with her hands and sobbed.

I cast around for words of sympathy, words that would offer comfort, but I couldn't find them.

She lowered her hands and moved closer to me. "You can go to bat for me with the sheriff, the newspapers, everybody. They'll listen to you. Don't let them sweep this under the rug. I want them to find Tammy's murderer and put him in jail. Is that too much to ask?"

"No. That doesn't seem like too much to ask," I said.

And it didn't.

CHAPTER SIX

JIM THOMPSON INVESTIGATED most of the Emerald Point cases for our county sheriff's department. For years he'd made a point of keeping Young Ned in the loop about the department's investigations into crime and suspected crime in the village. Now he did the same for me. When I telephoned him the next morning, he picked up at once when he heard I was on the line.

"Sorry, Mayor. Can't talk now. On my way down to Bailey's Motel. I'll have to get back to you."

No need to wait. Pauline had come in early to cover the office while I drove down to Glens Falls for an appointment with Stephanie Colvin at the *Post Standard*. Bailey's Motel was only a few blocks from my office. I could stop by there on the way.

As I drove through Emerald Point, I awarded our local business owners high marks. On this bright June morning, the town actually resembled the picture post card of it sold in our stores. To prepare for the summer tourist season, the merchants had primped and painted, hung new awnings, planted window boxes, even added benches along the sidewalks.

Our main street showcased the attractions common to any small lakeside town--souvenir shops, restaurants glamorized by names like *café* or *bistro*, a drugstore, a mom and pop grocery, gas stations and our very own post office and library. Off on a side street, I could see the red brick elementary school our students attended through Grade 6, after which they were bussed to Lake George Village for junior and senior high school.

Two large hotels and a sprinkling of motels within walking distance of downtown each offered a special something that helped lure tourists away from better known destinations on the lake. The Emerald Point Inn, run by John Roberts and his son Jack, emphasized old fashioned elegance. Phil Johnson's Beach House on the Point boasted a fabulous lakeside setting. The Pines, recently purchased by newcomers Peter and Jane Finch, provided guests with a pool and an attractive woodsy setting. The Iroquois cabins, owned by my friends Ramona and Deke Dolley, were comfortable and inexpensive. And Tom Bailey's Lakefront, where I was headed, featured the best view on the lake.

North of the village, elegant beachfront homes testified to the Point's wealthy past. Ranches and capes of more recent vintage dotted the streets radiating from the crescent-shaped business district. Our churches provided a mixed bag of services--worship on Sundays, Bingo and choir practice on week nights and lawn festivals and church fairs in season. Although our young people complained about the absence of a movie theater or drive-in, most of us ranked our little community a good place to live.

I was agreeing with that assessment as I drove up to Tom Bailey's motel that morning. To my surprise, I found two sheriff's cars, red lights flashing, angled in front of one of the rooms. I jumped out of my car.

The door to the room was ajar. I hesitated, then gave it a cautious push and stepped inside. Jim stood in front of the open door to the bathroom. Even in his civvies, the investigator personified most people's idea of a law enforcement official. He looked formidable, ready for whatever danger threatened. This morning he'd tucked a ski pole under his arm to leave his hands free for the fire extinguisher he was holding. A blue vinyl garbage can stood on the floor next to him.

Rick Cronin had positioned himself beside him. Rick had drawn his weapon and was pointing it into the bathroom. My heart skipped a beat. Rick was much too young to have to shoot somebody or--worse yet--get shot at himself.

"What the...? I couldn't see past Jim and the deputy into the obvious trouble spot, but I did a quick survey of the room. Unmade bed, rumpled white sheets, open suitcase, nothing out of the ordinary. A heavy-set, balding man, his face streaked with dried shaving cream, slumped in a chair next to a small desk. He wore dark suit pants, a white tee shirt and dress shoes with the laces dangling. A shirt and a pair of socks were lying across the bed behind him.

"Come on in, Mayor. Say hello to Mr. Webb here," Jim said, his light-hearted tone out-of-sync with what appeared to be a serious confrontation.

"What in the world's happening?" I asked. Despite his considerable bulk, the man looked so pale I thought he was going to pass out.

"Show her," Jim ordered him.

Webb reached for a camcorder lying on the desk next to him. He turned it around with the little screen facing toward me and pushed the play button.

The videotape showed the floor of a bathroom. If this guy hoped for a career as a videographer, he was headed for disappointment. His hands must have been shaking so violently he couldn't steady the camcorder. The way the tape bounced, he could have been filming an earthquake. The floor rose and sank, blurred and faded, until, suddenly, an image sprang to life, filling the little screen. In an amazingly clear close-up, a rattlesnake slithered into the frame. A very angry-looking rattlesnake, easily two feet long, gliding between the side of a tub and the bottom of a sink. As we watched, it stopped moving and shook its tail rattle at the camera.

"Good God. Did you make that tape here in this bathroom?" I said.

The man nodded, his eyes wide with the shock of seeing his visitor again. "I was barefoot, too. I looked down and it was crawling right at my foot."

"But there aren't supposed to be any around here, are there?" I asked Jim. One of those stupid questions you wish you could take back the minute they're out of your mouth.

"Hardly the point, now is it Mayor? It was in there this morning. Mr. Webb thought we wouldn't believe him so he made us this here documentary." He struggled to keep the corners of his mouth from betraying his amusement.

"But, how..."

"That fella must have come down from Tongue Mountain or thereabouts. Traveling here in the south, you might say."

"Where's the snake now, do you think?" I made a quick survey of everyone's shoes. Jim and the deputies wore leather boots--very heavy boots too, they looked to be--laced tight around their ankles. Mr. Webb wasn't wearing socks and his shoelaces were untied, but his cordovan wing tips with their thick soles seemed mighty sturdy. My open sandals promised no protection at all from an angry rattler.

Jim had followed my line of thought. "Climb right up on that chair over there, Mayor, if you'd feel better about things." He was grinning openly now.

I fought to hold onto a few shreds of dignity. I refused to let on how much I wanted to do exactly that.

"So where do you think the snake went, Mr. Webb?" I asked with as much poise as I could muster. I did a fast check of the corners of the room.

"I know it didn't get into the bedroom," the guest said. "When I looked down and saw it, I almost had a heart attack. I ran out of the bathroom and slammed the door. Then I started thinking about how nobody would believe me, how they'd say I was drunk or stoned. I went and got the camcorder out of my car. I pushed that door open real slow and easy, just wide enough to stick the camera in."

"That was brave of you. What would you have done if it crawled out at you?" I said.

"Got the hell outta there, of course. And that's what I'm about to do right now. Bailey better not charge me for the room, I'm telling you." Mr. Webb wiped the last of the shaving cream off his face and reached for his shirt.

"So if it was there then, where is it now?" I asked Jim.

"We don't see it in there now. Must be a hole somewhere, maybe around a water pipe," Jim said.

"Oh great. Well, I'd love to stay and help you guys find it, but I have official business to take care of." I was the one grinning now.

As I started to leave, Tom Bailey burst through the door. Tom had struggled for years in the motel business and this year--according to the local gossip mill--things were finally beginning to break for him. He was scowling as he surveyed the room and its occupant. "The switchboard operator called me. What the hell's going on here?"

Jim reprised the snake hunt and Mr. Webb delayed his departure long enough to replay the tape. I stayed to watch it again and to hear Tom's horrified gasp as the rattler appeared on the little screen. Not the best kind of advertising for a motel.

By the time Mr. Webb handed the tape over to Jim--as evidence, I guess--words like animal control and environmental conservation department were being tossed around.

"We'd best call in Paddy O'Connor. He's the animal control officer and this is why he gets the big bucks," Jim said.

"Right," I said. "I've seen his salary in the budget. As I recall, it would hardly cover a dose of anti-snake venom."

"Like yours and mine would?" Jim chuckled at his own joke. Local government jobs were notoriously poor-pay. It was a fact of life around here.

"Jim, I need to get going. Can you walk out with me? I want to ask you something, something serious."

We stepped outside and stood on the covered walkway running along the building. I switched gears fast.

"Tammy Stevenson. People are saying she was murdered. Is that true?" I asked.

Before Jim could answer Mr. Webb, still minus his socks, half stumbled through the door and sank down on a bench outside his room.

"Are you all right?" Jim asked him.

Webb had the green-around-the-gills look of man about to be sick. "Need some fresh air. I want to sit here a minute before I finish getting dressed. Don't mind telling you that damn thing scared me to death," he muttered.

I asked my question again. "Is it true, Jim? Was Tammy Stevenson murdered?"

Jim took my arm and guided me toward my car. "Looks that way. And now we got something else to consider. Somebody broke into the garage last night and jimmied open the glove compartment of her car. Bob Taggert told the mechanic he'd find the key and bring it in, but apparently whoever did it couldn't wait."

"Do they have any idea what could have been in there?"

"Nope. Thought there'd be no problem waiting for the key."

"I went to see Melissa yesterday. She was concerned about a pocketbook of Tammy's--a *Coach* bag. She said Tammy always carried it with her."

"She told one of the deputies that, too. I'm not sure exactly what a *Coach* bag is, but we didn't find anything like that. From her description, it wouldn't have fit in the glove compartment, anyway. Let me give you a call when I get back to the office." He opened my car door for me and turned back to Mr. Webb who was still slumped on the bench, staring at us with a dazed expression.

As I drove away, I was shaking my head over the many aspects of small town law enforcement. Here was our investigator taking time off from a murder case to cope with a rattlesnake in a motel bathroom. I could understand Melissa Taggert's frustration with Jim, but this was the real world and he sure managed to keep a lot of balls in the air at once.

CHAPTER SEVEN

I LEFT TOM'S motel and drove the fifteen miles to Glens Falls and the *Post Standard* offices. The building's brick façade with its freshly painted white trim glistened in the June sunshine. A receptionist seated behind a low counter in front took my name and buzzed Stephanie Colvin to announce my arrival. She waved me toward the editorial department, a large room with alcoves and cubbyholes along its edges, a mini-version of the *Washington Post* newsroom in *All the President's Men*. At this hour many of the desks were unoccupied and the clatter of typewriters, once the hallmark of a busy newsroom, had been replaced by the click of keyboards.

Stephanie--fashion magazines would describe her as a willowy blonde--stood up to greet me. From the first time I'd met her, I liked her style. She wrote feature articles for the paper and I was counting on her help with the community center we were planning. But the center wasn't first on the agenda today. Today I wanted to find out more about Tammy Stevenson's murder. Maybe, if I asked the right questions, Stephanie would tell me something I hadn't heard. She too was a relative newcomer to the area, but her position at the newspaper gave her access to the inside story on most happenings.

Stephanie pointed me to a chair in front of her desk and dispensed with formalities. "Let me guess. You've come to ask me about Tammy Stevenson."

I gulped, then gave her my best look of wide-eyed surprise. "Am I that transparent you can tell what I'm thinking before I say a word? How did you deduce that?"

"Or, maybe you've got something else on your mind." Was it my imagination or did she sound hopeful?

"I thought you might have heard things I haven't." I waited for her response--and waited some more. Like any good newspaperwoman, Stephanie respected her sources. All right. Mayors could play that game, too.

Stephanie shifted uncomfortably in her chair. "You've probably heard she was murdered. That's general knowledge now. Still, the feeling in the office is that we proceed with caution. There are some aspects of the case that make it a little tricky."

"Like what?"

"I'm not really in a position to say."

Not good enough. "Come on, Steph. I've told you things off the record. Don't you trust me enough to do the same?"

"I trust you, Loren, and this is definitely off the record. The rumor mill has it the girl was pregnant. Names are being floated rather indiscriminately. In fact, several influential men have been linked to her, but nobody knows anything for sure."

"Tricky is right."

"The feeling in the office is that we approach this very carefully."

"The feeling in the office? That's the second time you've used that expression. Whose feeling would that be?"

"I can give you several possibilities to choose from. There are those of us who think our esteemed editor has been asked to put a lid on this thing. Others figure he's just worried about opening a can of worms and riling one of his golfing buddies. Or, maybe the family wants to avoid publicity. Any or all of the above. Take your pick."

"I was under the impression the family *did* want publicity," I said.

"The mother does, anyway. That doesn't mean the others do," Stephanie said.

"Do you mean that she and the stepfather may not see eye to eye?"

"Possibly. Loren, this whole thing is a bit of a sticky wicket, as the Brits say. A sad mess. Keep me posted if you hear anything more."

Keep *her* posted? Hadn't I been the one asking the questions?

Stephanie leaned back in her chair, appearing more relaxed than she'd been since our conversation began.

"So what's new at the Point? Are you still kicking around your idea for some kind of museum?"

I got the message. Our discussion about Tammy was over. No point in pressing for more.

27

"Not a museum exactly. We're thinking of a community center with displays featuring various aspects of the lake."

"Sounds interesting. What would you include?"

I liked sounding out ideas with Stephanie.

"We're thinking about exhibits related to local history and environmental concerns. We'd include just about anything that would interest folks around here and bring in tourists as well. We've scheduled a meeting next week. I'll give you a call afterward and let you know how it goes."

THE REST OF the week filled up fast. Meetings with department heads and the finance committee took precedence over my concerns about Tammy Stevenson. I got my ducks in a row for a Chamber of Commerce meeting, juggled problems large and small with varying degrees of success and, all of a sudden, it was Friday noon and Pauline was bustling into the office ready for her shift.

"I have the Chamber meeting tonight and a couple of stops to make first," I told her. "If I take off right now and get some errands out of the way, I may be able to squeeze in a little R and R."

She nodded. "I'll be here 'til the usual time. Then I've got a date with Reggie to go for a fish fry. That'll be as much of a good time as I can handle."

"A date after all these years. That guy sure must have something," I said.

"Reggie's held up pretty well. He may be an old shoe, but he's a comfortable one."

For most of her working life Pauline had spent her days with the charismatic Ned, then had gone home to a guy even she saw as an old shoe. Did that shoe ever pinch, I wondered? And what kind of a shoe would she call me? Since I was feeling my way along in the job, I'd deliberately slowed down the *take no prisoners* style I'd honed in New York, but I knew I couldn't hold a candle to Young Ned. The man had oozed charm, pushed all the right buttons and held the town in the palm of his hand through years of political ups and downs. Even though Pauline never acted as if she found me wanting, she had to be making comparisons.

I had a few hours off before the meeting and Friday afternoon was the perfect time for a little more investigating. I knew exactly where to go next--I'd pay a visit to my young friend Josie Donohue.

I first met Josie and her mother Kate four years ago shortly after I moved to the Point. At that time Josie was a PIB, one of those *people in black* sometimes found on high school or college campuses, whose outlandish clothes and hair signal their unwillingness to be part of the mainstream. Now, at sixteen, Josie had mellowed a little, segued into denim and even conversed with adults on occasion. She was a little younger than Tammy had been, but if something happened to a teenager in Emerald Point, Josie knew every detail. The trick was getting her to let down her guard and tell me.

I picked up the latest editions of a couple of cooking magazines for Kate and headed over to the Donohue house. Kate's car was gone, but I spotted Josie curled up in a chair on the side porch, writing in a small notebook.

"Homework on a Friday afternoon?" I asked her.

"Get real, Lor." She tossed the notebook aside.

I handed her the magazines.

"I brought these for your mother, but I want to ask you something, too. What are they saying about Tammy Stevenson at school?"

"Most of the kids thought she skipped town last year. At least, that's what they're saying now. But nobody knew where she went."

"You mean even when her friends didn't hear from her, they still didn't think something might have happened to her?"

"She really didn't have any close friends, unless you count Todd Lewis. He was always following her around. Everybody figured Tammy could take care of herself. She always said she was gonna blow this place."

"Was life that bad for her here?"

"She fought with her mother all the time. Like, who doesn't? But Tammy was probably doing mucho stuff her mother didn't like."

"Such as?"

"What's that thing they do on Court TV--take the fifth? I take the fifth on that question." She gave me an exaggerated wink.

"Okay. New subject. I know she had a stepfather and a stepbrother. Did she have trouble with them, do you think?"

"Never heard she did. Rob got his own apartment a while ago and Old Bob had kinda given up on her, I guess."

"So what did she want to get away from?"

"She thought her life sucked. Men were always hittin' on her, you know? She was fed up."

"What men?"

"A lot of 'em. Fathers of kids she babysat for, guys in the restaurant where she worked one time, a teacher even. At least, that's what Todd said."

"That's a serious accusation to make, kiddo, especially against a teacher."

Josie rolled her eyes.

"Hey, I'm not the one who made the moves. You want to pretend that stuff doesn't happen, Lor?"

"No. I'm asking. You're telling."

"Tammy got propped by a lot of older guys."

"Propped?"

"You know, propositioned?"

"For sex?"

Josie snorted in disgust. We'd been friends for a long time. She saw no reason to coddle me now just because I was mayor.

"Like what else could I mean? Some of our top-drawer citizens made moves on her."

"You mean like people here in town?"

Another snort.

"Sure. She could have waitressed a lot of places or worked in the shops. You know, the usual jobs kids get around here. But she always said the jobs came with too big a price tag. I figured when she took off, it meant she'd had enough."

I felt a wave of sympathy for Tammy Stevenson. How could any teenage girl be better off on her own with no family or friends to lean on?

Unless, of course, she hadn't planned to leave alone.

CHAPTER EIGHT

WHEN I ARRIVED at the Emerald Point Inn that night, I found the Chamber meeting in full swing. Thirty of our local business owners had gathered in the Inn's back dining room to listen to a talk by Don Morrison, a member of a group called Bateaux Below. I tiptoed in and slipped into the empty chair next to Kate Donohue.

Kate, freed from catering responsibilities for the evening, was wearing what she called *people clothes*. The bright yellow slacks and top played up her dark eyes and blunt-cut black hair to perfection.

"I've had to fight to hold that chair for you. Why are you so late?" she whispered.

"I didn't think I was. What have I missed?" I said.

She nodded toward the speaker.

"Don's not as mellow as usual tonight. The Bateaux Below people are up in arms about zebra mussels. Ugly little critters. You've missed the slides, so you have to take my word for it."

Shortly after I took office, the Emerald Point Chamber of Commerce had voted to move their monthly meetings to Friday nights and add a social hour. The idea paid off. Attendance had gone up immediately as members rated the chance to combine business with pleasure a definite plus.

The program for the evening had been arranged by Bateaux Below, a group committed to preserving the treasure-trove of sunken ships on the bottom of the lake. Don was reviewing the organization's recent activities.

"...Our main interest is still diving and maintaining the Bateaux sites," he was saying. "We've got a priceless heritage, here, dating back to the French and Indian War, and we want to stay on top of it. Right now, as a good-will gesture, we're doing our annual spring cleanup. That's where I've been today, down where our divers found the zebra mussels."

There was a rustling in the room as the audience buzzed among themselves. People here had been reading about the menace of zebra mussels in other lakes. So far, Lake George had escaped them.

"We thought we were safe," Don continued. "After all our struggles with milfoil, we thought we'd lucked out with the zebra mussels. The alkaline content of the water seemed to be creating an inhospitable environment for them."

Someone from the front row interrupted him. "You found 'em down in the Village, didn't you? And you didn't find very many. What difference does it make to us?" I recognized the voice of George Tyler, Emerald Point's leading xenophobe.

After countless exchanges over the years, Don had perfected a technique for dealing with people like George. "I don't have to tell you this, Mr. Tyler. You know the score. The lake is important to all of us. We have to take care of it."

Don's words were right on target. Our economy, like that of our neighbors around here, depended on the lake. A few miles south of us, Lake George Village attracted visitors with its Million Dollar Beach--a reference to an initial price tag people still talked about--and a vast conglomeration of motels and restaurants, shops and arcades, lake steamers and boat rentals. History buffs toured the restored *Fort William Henry*, checked out the statues and digs at Battleground Park and refreshed their memories about French and Indian War battles. Tourists flocked to the discount stores south of town and to the Great Escape, a theme park a few miles beyond that. Was it any wonder that a small community like Emerald Point struggled for its identity?

"Don't know why we're wasting time on this crap." George Tyler had found his voice and was on his feet again, addressing the group. "Gambling is where the money is. There's going to be changes coming, relaxation of a lot of the old rules and we should be ready to take advantage. That's what we should be talking about, not those stupid zebra mussels."

"Pie in the sky," Tom Bailey shouted as he jumped up and glared across the room at George. "You think we could ever pull off something like that? People here want to gamble, they go to Saratoga."

George sputtered out the beginning of a response, but Tom moved too quickly for him. He shoved his chair back, scraping it across the floor, blotting out George's words. "I don't know about the rest of you, but I'm ready for a drink."

His comment brought the meeting to an unceremonious close.

Kate and I joined the group moving toward the bar.

"Ready for a wine?" I asked her.

"Am I ever. It's a treat to be a guest at a party, instead of the one doing the work."

Although most of the Chamber meetings were held at the Emerald Point Inn, other area restaurant owners sometimes pitched in to provide the refreshments. Tonight Phil Johnson and one of his waiters from the Beach House on the Point were circulating with a tray of picture-perfect seafood.

"You know that's Rob Taggert, don't you?" Kate said in my ear.

Rob, I realized, must be Bob Taggert's son, the one Pauline had mentioned. Not bad looking--mid-twenties, probably a former athlete, but now out of shape, running to fat.

Kate and I, carrying our glasses of wine, followed him like bloodhounds on the scent. Before I could fight my way through the melee surrounding Rob and his tray, Jack Roberts, the Inn's manager, took my arm and pulled me aside.

"Loren, hi. I was afraid you weren't coming."

I'd known Jack since my teenage visits here. He'd grown up in Emerald Point, called it home until after he graduated from college, but his clothes, his manner, even his new-style glasses set him apart from the locals. His single status and his dark good looks prompted many of the hotel's women guests to consider spicing up their vacations with a romantic fling.

"It's great to see you. Join me for a drink upstairs later?" He leaned into me and spoke with just the right note of urgency. His smile had been known to melt a woman's firmest resolve.

"Upstairs?"

"Like, on my deck. Perfect spring evening. Full moon over the water."

"It's freezing out, and I didn't see any moon when I drove over here."

He pressed closer. "Totally wrong setting for it. The Emerald Point Inn guarantees satisfaction even if there isn't a moon."

"A slogan I suspect you've always lived up to," I said, trying to be flip but feeling my face burn. I moved quickly away.

A group of motel owners--the Inn Crowd, we called them-- stood chatting in a corner of the bar.

Ramona Dolley made a place for me in the circle. Someone had once called Ramona and her husband Deke a matched pair, and it was an apt description. Both short and a little chunky, with hair either by accident or design an identical shade of gray, they reminded me of the grandparents in a set of dolls I'd once loved.

"Join us, Loren, but no murder talk. I hear they buried that poor girl today, or at least what was left of her. But that's not gonna be the end of it. Melissa's planning a memorial service for her next week. Like business here wasn't bad enough, anyway, we got to keep reminding people."

The Dolleys ran the Iroquois, a ten-unit motel on Route 9N. Last summer, Ramona had confided, they'd never once lit their No Vacancy sign.

"Have you met Peter and Jane Finch? I was telling them you were knocking yourself out to help us local business folks."

Peter and Jane were attractive forty-somethings who'd moved up from Lake George Village the year before. The rumor circulated that Jeannie Spenser, Ramona's daughter and a sharp Lake George realtor, had negotiated a complicated deal for them on the motel they'd bought just north of town. Peter and Jane had re-landscaped around the pool and added a small restaurant in the hope of giving their guests what they called the *full service experience.*

"I told them you were thinking of joining us in the hospitality business, Loren, that you were talking about opening your own Bed and Breakfast," Ramona said.

"I did consider it, but I've put that idea on hold for now," I told the Finches. "After I started fixing up my grandfather's house and realized how much everything cost, I figured I'd better check out some other possibilities."

Peter Finch turned toward his wife "That's what you want me to do, isn't it Jane, check out other possibilities?" His voice took on an ugly tone.

I glanced down at his hands. The skin around his fingernails was chewed raw. As he spoke, he rubbed his left hand nervously up and down his leg. The long northern New York winters combined with a big mortgage could make people in the motel business mighty jumpy.

I tried to smooth things over.

"Well, my case is different. I made a move into politics and that kind of sidetracked me," I said.

"Sidetracked. I could tell you about sidetracked." To my surprise, Peter Finch slammed his empty glass down on the table next to where he was standing, turned on his heel and stalked off.

Chapter Nine

BEFORE ANY OF us had time to react to Peter's strange behavior, we heard angry voices coming from the bar. George and a group of men standing near him were engaged in a heated argument. Another exchange about gambling.

George, frustrated by his failure to get the subject discussed at the meeting, was shouting at Don Morrison.

"We got people from here running up to that casino at Montreal. We need to get the Canadians coming back down here the way they used to," he yelled.

Don made an obvious effort to keep his cool.

"Blame the exchange rate for that, George. Too expensive for them to vacation down here now."

"They'd get down here fast enough if we had gambling. Wouldn't matter what the exchange rate was. They're talking about building casinos in New York State. Why can't we get one built right here?" George demanded.

Don shook his head. "You know why, George. Native Americans are the only ones can offer gambling, and only on their reservations. Tribal lands--that's the key. None of the tribes made permanent settlements around here."

"Enough of them fought in the battles for the lake. That should count for something," George insisted.

Once again, Tom Bailey jumped into the argument. "You're out of line, George. Shut up about this stuff. This here's a social hour. Nobody's on the warpath tonight."

Kate moved in close behind me. "What's wrong with these people? Let's find a table and sit down before we get caught in a brawl."

I made my excuses and followed Kate to a small table near the window.

"Did Josie tell you I stopped by your house this afternoon? She told me some rea'' 'sturbing things about Tammy Stevenson."

"Yes. I've he..u them, too. I complain about Josie sometimes, but it sounds like Melissa really had her hands full with Tammy."

I touched her arm. I seldom talked about how much I'd wanted children, even to close friends like Kate, but I always imagined them as adorable, well-behaved cherubs, not rebellious teenagers. Kate could identify with Melissa Taggert's heartache far better than I could.

John Roberts, Jack's father, stopped by our table. Years ago, John had been considered one of the town's shrewdest businessmen, but recent years had taken their toll. Now frail and in poor health, he'd turned over most of the business to Jack.

"Evenin,' girls. Be nice if we could get those guys to find a bateaux or two up here by us. Maybe even some of them cannon balls used to be out around Diamond Island, anything to put our town on the map."

"You're right, John, as long as they don't find zebra mussels," I said.

He chuckled in agreement.

As John strolled away, Don Morrison dropped into an empty chair at our table.

"Sorry about the argument," he said, glancing back at the group he'd just left. "That George can always get me going. I came to say I'll be diving the bateaux site again Sunday, Loren, if you want to stop by."

Even in street clothes, Don looked like a diver--tall and rangy with a thick growth of blond hair, still tousled from his day outdoors, his cheeks burned either by the sun or the wind to the vivid pink of a Lake George sunset. He was somewhere in his forties and, although his heavy blond beard made him little hairy for my taste, I rated him a definite *okay*.

"I might do just that. We're thinking of having a display on the bateaux in our new center. I'd like to refresh my memory about them," I said.

His face lit up. "Good idea. Emerald Point is right at the midpoint of the lake. Even if you don't have the best preserved bateaux up here, the ones scattered around on the bottom are as much yours as anyone else's."

An amateur historian as well as a diver, Don possessed a wealth of facts and figures on anything to do with the lake. I loved his enthusiasm, but, right then, I was too tired to listen. I excused myself with a promise to meet him at the site on Sunday.

Kate was in no hurry to leave. "I'll hang around a while longer, Loren. Call you tomorrow," she said.

Jack was talking business at the bar as I went by. Several years before, with his father's health failing, Jack had moved back to the Point and taken over many of his father's duties. Still, Mr. Roberts hung on, reluctant to announce his retirement.

As I was putting on my coat in the lobby, Jack caught up with me. "You're not going to stay?" He sounded disappointed, as if he was about to protest, to urge me to change my mind, even to suggest we get together another time.

"I'm beat. I think I'll go along."

"Well, good night then," he said as he pulled open the Inn's massive front door.

Damn him sometimes. Years ago we'd racked up a few dates, a few near-misses, even a few tears (mine, definitely not his). But that was over. I valued his friendship, needed his help in promoting Emerald Point. I could do without the game playing.

I was content with my life here, at least for the most part, I was content. But sometimes, like tonight, when I walked out of the hotel alone, a feeling of loneliness overwhelmed me and I wondered if I was crazy not to move back to New York.

CHAPTER TEN

I DROVE HOME slowly, mindful of the wine, my mood as bleak as the overcast sky. I met only two or three cars as I headed up 9N. Cold spring nights could be dreary at the lake. Most of my neighbors along the road had shut off their yard lamps and retired. Only a few dimly lighted windows, usually in the bedrooms of the houses I passed, broke the monotony. I pulled into the parking area behind the house.

I parked my Saab under a favorite maple and picked my way slowly along the slate path that led to the back door. The pole lamp, usually a cheery presence in the yard, had gone out. Dead bulb, I supposed. My feeling of isolation intensified. Silly, I scolded myself, it's only a burned out bulb. You can replace it in the morning.

I took small, careful steps on the rough slates. I could see the dark mass of the lake at the front of the house and hear the steady beat of waves, whipped by a strong north wind. Warm weather had been promised, just not quite yet.

I'd almost reached the house when I heard the slam of a car door. I glanced toward the sound. A figure visible only as an elongated shadow detached itself from the privet hedge and moved toward me. I jumped back, staggered, and caught myself before I fell. My heart pounded as I turned to face the man who'd appeared out of nowhere.

Warning signals went off in my brain. It was too late for visitors.

"What..." I stammered. "Who are you? What do you want?"

I dug deep in my pocket, fumbling for my keys. If I could punch him hard with the keys sticking out of my fist, I might slow him enough to beat him to the back door.

"Didn't mean to scare you, Mayor." The words rang false. The man towered over me. His heavy dark clothes and the knit cap pulled low on his forehead intensified the sense of danger he projected. Even if I aimed the keys just right, I wouldn't have much chance of stunning him with a punch. He moved nearer to me. I smelled beer and cigarettes on his breath as he brought his face closer --too close--to mine.

"Who are you?" I asked again. I tried to keep any trace of fright out of my voice, but didn't think I succeeded.

"Just want to talk to you a minute. I was at my friend's place up the road when I saw you go by. I want you to forget that crazy idea of Melissa's about helping her find out who killed Tammy. She's buried now. We gotta put this thing behind us and move on."

"I don't know who you are or what you're talking about," I said.

"I know you came to see Melissa. She says you agreed to go to bat for her with the sheriff and the newspaper. I'm tellin' you, it's a lousy idea. Don't do it."

The light began to dawn.

"Wait a minute. Are you Bob Taggert?" I asked.

"You got that right. And I'm sick to death of worrying about that kid and what happened to her. We've spent long enough on that, I say. And I'm even sicker of seeing what all this has done to her mother. Now that we know, I want to be shut of it, get life back to normal. Can you understand that?"

"Yes, I can understand that." I spoke as calmly as I could.

"We got kids together, you know, Melissa and me. She might better pay some attention to them."

He was probably right about that, but this was hardly the way to convince me. I straightened my shoulders and glared at him.

"I'll talk to you in my office any time you want to come in, Mr. Taggert, but you've got no business coming to my home this late. Unless you're trying to intimidate me."

"Hey, if I want to intimidate you, I can think of better ways to do it." He spit the words at me as he moved even closer.

I got a blast of the beer smell again. I thought he was raising his hand to hit me. I closed my fingers around my keys. Suddenly, he turned on his heel and went striding away from me toward a car half-hidden by trees on the opposite side of the street. He shut the door hard and gunned the motor before he drove off. Bob Taggert wanted me to know he was one tough customer.

I believed him. I wasn't going to wait for him to come back. My hand shook, but I had the key in the lock of the back door in seconds. I crossed the little entrance way in two strides and unlocked the kitchen door. Once inside, I threw the bolt and snapped the heavy metal chain in place, grateful to Pete, my handyman, for the extra hardware he'd put on the door for me. I was shaking harder than I wanted to acknowledge. Bob Taggert had scared me, no doubt about it.

I kept my jacket on as I turned on the lights in the kitchen and living room. Quickly, I checked the locks on the front door and on each of the downstairs windows. All okay. I was walking back into the kitchen when I saw a flash of light at the rear of the house--headlights. A car pulling into the parking area. Maybe he'd decided to come back.

I looked around for a weapon and settled on a baseball bat standing in the corner of the kitchen. Bob Taggett had almost a hundred pounds on me but, with the phone on the table in the front hall and my pepper spray upstairs on my nightstand, the bat was the only thing within reach.

I eased up to the side of the kitchen window and lifted the curtain enough to peer out. Someone had come down the walk and was standing facing away from me near the pole lamp. I could make out the outline of a back, but that was all. I tightened my grip on the bat. Suddenly, I jumped back, blinded by a flash of light. The outside lamp had been turned on, the one with the burned out bulb. Before I could figure out how that had happened, someone pounded hard on the outer door.

I froze against the window casing trying not to move or make a sound.

The knock came again, even louder this time.

"Loren! Loren, it's me." It was Kate's voice.

Relief flooded through me. I set down the bat and unlocked the kitchen door. I was still shaky enough to check once more before I opened the second door.

"Kate? Is it really you?"

"Uh oh. Were you expecting someone else maybe?" As she stepped inside, I was enveloped in a rush of cold air.

"The outside light. I thought it was burned out." I tried to sound matter-of-fact.

"I tightened the bulb and it came back on. Guess it was just loose."

I pulled off my jacket and threw it at a kitchen chair.

"Coffee? A drink? I'm so glad you came," I said.

41

"I decided to hell with guys who don't know enough to go home."

I reached for the coffee maker. I could feel the knots inside me loosen, feel myself begin to unwind. Kate and I had some of our best conversations like this, late at night in my kitchen over coffee and sinfully delicious treats I'd brought home from her restaurant the day before. Move back to New York? What had I been thinking of?

CHAPTER ELEVEN

AFTER KATE LEFT, I fought hard to keep thoughts of Bob Taggert at bay, but they came rushing back. Maybe I should have told her about the encounter, I thought, but I'd wanted time to think. Kate would have heard me out--and insisted I report Bob Taggert to the sheriff's department at once.

And maybe that was exactly what I should do--talk to Jim Thompson without making too big a deal of it. But one thing I was sure of--Jim, committed first and foremost to law enforcement, would do what he thought was right. Even if I urged him not to overreact, he might not listen to me. I could easily be getting Bob Taggert in trouble. Did I really want to do that? Here were two people coping with a tragedy so great I couldn't even imagine what life must be like for them. They might not be using the best judgment, but they didn't need me adding to their problems.

Saturday morning, as I lingered over coffee in my kitchen, I decided to let that decision stand, at least for the time being. Somewhere I had a report on the Submerged Heritage Preserve I'd brought home to read. If I was going to meet Don at the bateaux site on Sunday, I should check it out.

I skimmed the report quickly. I already knew the basic facts. What he'd be showing me would be the Wiawaka bateaux, also called the Sunken Fleet of 1758, near the southern end of the lake. Another day, I'd check out the Land Tortoise, a 1758 gun battery, also part of the preserve, discovered by side-scan sonar a few miles north of Lake George Village.

I found it easy to visualize replicas of these sunken ships in our center. The bateaux, or longboats, were used by both British and French to transport soldiers and supplies. The Land Tortoise wasn't a bateaux but a radeau, a class of military vessel unique to Lake George and Lake Champlain in the eighteenth century. The radeau--

43

the word meant raft in French--was the sole survivor of a dozen floating artillery platforms built by provincial volunteers to be used against the French. I double-checked the dimensions. The radeau, over fifty feet long and sixteen to eighteen feet wide, had been larger than our Village Building.

I was pouring myself the last cup of coffee in the carafe when Josie arrived.

"It's Saturday. You're up early," I said.

"I've come to report."

"Josie, you're the best. Want a soda?"

"Whatever."

I reached into the refrigerator and handed her a can of her favorite wakeup beverage.

"You wanted to know about Tammy. The coroner finished whatever he had to do and the family had the burial yesterday."

"I heard that, too. I was surprised. I thought her mother would want some kind of funeral service."

"She does. She's planning a memorial or something for the first of the week. I guess people can go to that. I'll keep you posted."

As soon as Josie left, I called Jim Thompson. People thought nothing of calling me on weekends. Why should I wait for Monday for an update?

"I talked to Melissa," I said when I got him on the line. "Then I heard the coroner released Tammy body. Any leads on who killed her?"

"We're trying to piece things together. It'll take time. Here's what I've told the Taggerts: her skull was fractured, she was hit. Hit hard and more than once. She'd been dead a long time, as much as a year. You see why we could never trace her car. But, until now, there was no indication she was a victim of foul play, not any place around here at least."

"I assume you'd filed a missing persons report."

"Sure. Nothing from that, either. Nobody reported seeing her after June second of last year. That was the night she had the argument with her mother and left the house. She was probably killed soon after that. Officially, she was considered a runaway."

"So, off the record, what did you think had happened to her?"

He hesitated. I could sense him deciding how much to divulge.

"Off the record, Tammy Stevenson was a kid with problems and she created problems for other people. She caused trouble, and I mean trouble with a capital T. I wouldn't have been surprised if somebody had paid her way out of town."

"Exactly what does that mean?"

"There were rumors. She played games, mind games and body games both, if you take my meaning. She worked as a chambermaid, was said to perform other services in motel rooms besides cleaning them."

"Are you implying prostitution?"

"Nothing that formal. More freelance, I'd say. But I think a lot of people around here were glad to see the last of her."

"Her stepfather for one?"

"Probably, but that doesn't make him the bad guy. He put up with a lot of crap from her, more than most stepparents--parents either, for that matter--would have stood for."

"So, what other people?"

Another hesitation.

"She worked in several motels around here. Maybe you could have asked Tom Bailey, if he wasn't so shook up about that rattler at his place. Or Peter Finch, or your friend Ramona."

"Tammy worked for all of them?"

"And more. She did chambermaid work for a lot of motels. Never lasted long in any job. I'm telling you, the girl was trouble."

"But mind games? What does that mean?"

Jim sighed deep and long.

"I hate it when you make me spell it all out for you, Mayor. Like maybe she told guys she was pregnant, tried to get money out of them for an abortion. Or maybe she asked them to pay her way out of town."

"Was she pregnant?"

"Hard to be sure now, but it doesn't look like it."

"Does her mother know any of this?"

"In this town? She's got to have heard plenty. But she doesn't let on to me. She probably doesn't want to believe the stories, especially now."

"So the case is complicated," I said.

Another sigh from Jim.

"I find most things are, Mayor, at least in my line of work."

What an indictment. Tammy Stevenson had been just seventeen years old when she was murdered--a beautiful young girl with an exaggerated sense of her own cleverness, involved in a dangerous game. Jim had accused her of playing both mind and body games. That, too, was a vague phrase. I still wasn't sure exactly what it meant, but I didn't like the sound of it. I didn't like the sound of it at all.

CHAPTER TWELVE

SUNDAY AFTERNOON I drove along the east side of the lake and turned onto the road leading to Wiawaka Holiday House, just opening for the summer.

I didn't have to be a genius to figure out that plans for diving the bateaux site that day had been scrapped. No sign of boats or divers. I parked near Wiawaka's main building and walked down to the shore. Don and a man I didn't recognize stood huddled against a fierce north wind, gazing out at the choppy water.

"No diving today?" I asked them.

"Too rough. Too cold. Too few showed up. Those are our excuses. Take your pick," Don said.

His companion extended his hand.

"I'm Colby Ledyard. We're heading to Vic's. Come with us and we'll talk there."

Vic's Bar, a loud, smoky, gathering place, wasn't exactly my favorite hangout, but I'd been too tired Friday night to ask all my questions about the bateaux. I agreed to follow them to Vic's.

"Beer okay? I'll get us a pitcher," Don said as we walked in. As Colby and I sat down at one of the tables, he ambled off toward the bar.

Colby Ledyard looked to be older than many divers, maybe sixty or more, but a trim athletic sixty. I wasn't surprised when he told me he was a professor at a college in Albany. Even in jeans and a leather jacket, Colby came across as tweedy and professorial. I almost expected him to pull a pipe out of his pocket and add to the cloud of smoke hanging over the room.

"So exactly what are you planning to do with this information on the preserve?" he asked me as we waited for Don to return.

"We want to do displays on the lake--contour maps, models, exhibits of various kinds. Got any ideas for me?"

"Only that you leave the bateaux out of it."

He was kidding, wasn't he? So why was his expression deadly serious?

"Excuse me?"

"Do us a favor and leave the bateaux out of your plans. We've got too many people diving those sites anyway. If we attract more of them, we lose more artifacts--and they're irreplaceable."

"But I thought the sites were well controlled. You have to be a certified diver to dive them don't you?"

"That doesn't mean squat. Too much publicity on the sites leads to losses."

"Why can't publicity work the other way, make people realize how important the artifacts are?" I said.

Colby, his face flushed, was revving up to answer when Don returned juggling three glasses and a full pitcher of beer. He poured a glass for each of us and slid into the chair at my right.

Don took a long swallow of beer, clunked his glass down and looked from one of us to the other, making a slow appraisal of our faces.

"So, I see you two are into it already. Colby been telling you he's against publicizing the underwater sites, has he?"

"Why? Are you about to tell me the same thing yourself?" I bristled.

Apparently, Don was enough of a diplomat not to walk into that one.

"I share Colby's concerns, of course. Everybody who cares about the lake's artifacts worries about vandalism and thievery. But there are treasures under that water and people have a right to know about them."

Colby snapped his answer at both of us.

"They can know all they want if they keep their trophy-picking hands to themselves."

"He's right about that part of it," Don agreed. "We coined a slogan a couple years ago to help educate folks--*Take only photographs; leave only bubbles.*"

"Catchy," I said.

Colby scowled again.

"Not catchy enough, unfortunately. We've lost too much already. For example, folks remember seeing cannon balls up around

Diamond Island--there was a supply depot up there, you know. They're gone now, all of them."

"Yes, somebody mentioned that at a meeting recently," I said.

"I agree we need to safeguard discoveries." Don spoke slowly, his reasonable tones a contrast to Colby's angry bark. "The bateaux are a priceless record of the French and Indian War period. We can't afford to lose them."

"As I understand it, they were sunk deliberately to safeguard them from the French," I said.

"Right. More than two hundred fifty sunk in the fall of 1758 alone. Secured for the winter that way. They raised most of 'em the following spring but some, like the Wiawaka Seven over where you went this afternoon, slid into deep water out of reach. Sinking wasn't a precise art, you know," Don said.

"What if they were brought to the surface and put in a museum somewhere?" I asked, already thinking how the remnants of an actual bateaux would enhance our center.

"No way," both men said together.

"Much too fragile," Don said.

"Been tried. Didn't work. They'd fall apart," Colby added.

Finally, I'd stumbled onto something they agreed on.

With Colby helping, Don launched into an explanation of the problems involved in sinking the bateaux. He painted a vivid picture of the men's exhausting struggles in the freezing water as they loaded heavy rocks--sinking stones, the provincials called them--into the newly built longboats, then drove holes into the hulls.

I took in every word, already visualizing a diorama with life sized figures and replicas of the boats. Great human interest stuff for our center.

As Colby and Don went on talking, I found myself distracted by a tall, burly man in a dark jacket who'd joined a group at the bar. His face was turned away as he stood talking to the bartender, but something about his height and the shape of his shoulders seemed familiar. The man at the bar could easily be Bob Taggert. I wasn't afraid of him, I told myself. I just didn't want another confrontation.

I interrupted Don to ask, "That man in the dark blue jacket. Do you know his name?"

Both men glanced over and shook their heads.

I turned my back on the bar and resolved not to look again.

"So, tell me more about the bateaux."

Don was happy to oblige.

"Think about what it was like raising them in the spring. Imagine diving into that water with the ice barely gone out of the lake, lugging those sinking stones up from twenty feet below the surface."

I gave an involuntary shiver. I tried to concentrate on what he was telling me. Maybe I should have reported Bob Taggert to the sheriff. It wasn't too late. I could talk to Jim tomorrow.

When I looked back at the bar, the man I was obsessing about had disappeared. As much as I hated to admit it, I felt a wave of relief.

Chapter Thirteen

A short time later I thanked Don and Colby and said good-bye.

"I'll keep you guys posted," I told them.

"If you quote me, be sure you spell my name right," Don said with a wink as he helped me on with my jacket.

"That goes for me, too," Colby added.

Not as adamant as he'd been at first, I noted. Maybe the change of tone meant he'd thawed toward the idea of the display.

As I pulled into my yard, the outside lamp, miraculously restored to life, gleamed in the fading light. The lake was calm; the wind had finally gone down. A small boat putt-putted by. The summer people were trickling back for weekends now. Soon, before we knew it, the season would be in full swing.

When I walked into the house, I spotted the bright red '1' on my answering machine: The message was from Kate: "Loren. Come over and have dinner with me tonight."

Kate didn't have to ask me twice. I started for the door, then stopped myself. For one of Kate's special meals, I could at least change clothes. I ran upstairs and replaced my flannel shirt with a blue cable-knit sweater just the right weight for a cool spring night and added some silver earrings with matching blue stones. A dinner guest anyone would be glad to feed.

Kate's home was two blocks from the little coffee shop where she'd recently moved her catering headquarters and only a short drive from my house. As she opened the door to my knock, she gave a little squeal of surprise.

"Loren, I didn't think you'd get my message in time, so I padded the guest list. I'm really glad you came."

I handed her a bottle of Merlot I'd brought along and she ushered me into her big country kitchen. A couple I knew slightly lounged against the u-shaped counter, sipping wine from Kate's crystal wine glasses.

"I think you know the Treadwells, Allison and Ralph," she said.

Allison Treadwell nodded a hello as Ralph and I shook hands. Allison, a big woman--Rubenesque might be the politically correct term--was all in black with a pretty multi-colored silk scarf arranged around her shoulders. Ralph muttered a greeting and leaned back against the counter.

"Why are you cooking on your day off?" I asked Kate.

She pulled a tray of fresh baked rolls from the oven and tumbled them into a napkin-lined basket.

"Same reason you weren't home this afternoon when I called you, I bet. Town business even on Sunday?"

Before I could admit my guilt, Allison walked over to me.

"My friend Melissa says you're going to help her get some action on Tammy," she announced.

I replied with a low murmur. Even supposedly capable public officials fell back on undecipherable mutterings when the need arose.

Allison didn't let my lack of response deter her.

"Not that I necessarily agree with Melissa. Now that she knows Tammy's dead, she might better get on with her life, but she won't listen."

Exactly what Bob Taggert had said. I wondered if he made a habit of discussing his wife with their friends.

Before I could decide how to respond to Allison, Kate motioned us into the dining room. The table sparkled with her best china and silver. The main course, a turkey tetrazzini loaded with hunks of succulent turkey, required our complete attention.

After we all swore we couldn't eat another bite, Kate jumped up to clear the table.

"Stay where you are. I have this down to a science," she said and disappeared into the kitchen.

Allison seized the moment.

"Exactly what are you planning to do for Melissa?" she demanded.

I took my time answering.

"I'm not sure she'll need my help. I expect the sheriff's department will tell her something before long."

"Except they won't. Melissa doesn't think they'll get anywhere. She's counting on you." Her voice took on a strident tone.

Ralph glanced from one of us to the other, apparently ready to add his opinion.

Kate's dinner table was not the place for an argument. I beat a hasty retreat to the kitchen.

Kate needed only a quick look at my face to realize something was amiss.

"Uh oh. Allison, I bet," she said.

I made a gesture of dismissal.

"A minor disagreement. Not to worry," I responded.

I slipped into Kate's downstairs bathroom just as Allison carried a few dirty dishes to the sink. I saw her glance around, apparently looking for me and a chance to continue our exchange. Melissa and Bob Taggert weren't the only ones anxious to give me their views on Tammy Stevenson's murder. This was a hot button topic and it looked as if I'd be hearing about it every place I went.

Chapter Fourteen

"JOSIE IN HER room? Okay if I run up and say hello?" I asked Kate as soon as I came out of the bathroom. Josie had chosen to skip dinner with company--her usual practice. I needed a time out myself.

Allison gave me a dirty look and flounced back into the dining room.

I sprinted for the stairs. I knew the location of the sanctum sanctorum from other visits, but I would never presume to enter unannounced. I knocked lightly on the Phish poster taped to the outside of the bedroom door.

"Whatever," Josie's voice called.

I took that for permission to open the door. Josie was sitting up in bed, writing in the same little notebook she'd had with her on the hammock. She motioned me in.

"You sick or hiding out?" I asked.

"Both. Just thinking about those people makes me barf."

"You didn't approve the guest list. I'm hurt."

She tossed the notebook aside.

"Not you, Lor. You know better than that. But Mrs. Treadwell's down there, isn't she? She's a piece of work."

I couldn't bring myself to disagree.

"And Mr. T.'s a real dork. He tried to get me to babysit for his kids after Tammy Stevenson left town, but I wouldn't do it."

"Tammy babysat for the Treadwells?"

"Yeah. She sat for them two summers, anyway, and a lot of weekends. She wanted to buy a car in the worst way. Put up with all kinds of crap from Mr. T. to do it."

"Josie, what are you saying? Are you accusing him of something?"

"Of hittin' on her. Sure. He was the one I was talking about the other day. Of course, that wasn't anything new for Tammy. It happened all the time."

Before I could ask more, we heard the sound of the doorbell.

"Lucky you. New guests." Josie sank back against her pillows.

"A nice change of pace for us tonight, kiddo. I get to party hearty and all you get is a good night's sleep," I said.

"Like I care. I definitely got the best deal. Throw this in the nightstand drawer for me, will ya?" She handed me the little book and slid farther down into the bed.

"Is this your diary? You must really trust your mother if you don't hide it better than that." I picked up the book and slipped it into the drawer.

"Yeah. Right. Like I'd be that stupid. If I don't want her to know something, I write it in code."

"You what? Josie, you never cease to amaze me."

When she didn't answer, I switched off the light and left the room.

Downstairs, I found Kate greeting new guests in the front hall.

"Loren, I think you know Matt Tremont and Mary."

Matt, the dowser, stepped forward and extended his hand. A short, stocky man of French Canadian descent, he was dressed as he'd been at the car-raising in a heavy wool sport shirt and corduroy slacks. Adirondackers weren't tricked into thinking summer had come by what the calendar said.

"Yes, I saw Matt the other day when they were raising Tammy Stevenson's car. I'd never seen that done before," I told Mary as we walked into the living room.

"Matt could have found it for them before this if they'd asked him. He's found a lot of things for people in the lake. He's a gold mine of information about anything on the bottom," Mary said.

"A gold mine?" I asked with a smile.

Matt Tremont had crinkly eyes and the tanned, heavily lined face of a man who'd spent long days in the sun.

"I've never found any gold, I'm sorry to say. I've found pickups that went through the ice, a half dozen motors and an assortment of boats and anchors. But I'll take a crack at anything you got in mind. What are you looking for?"

"Thanks, but nothing right now. We're thinking about creating a display on the bateaux for our community center. I forget how much else may be down there on the bottom," I said.

"Sure. Boats aren't the only things, you know. There's broken glassware and silver from the old hotels, furniture, all kinds of great junk. Maybe even Georgie the lake monster."

"And you can find all these things by dousing?" I said.

He grinned. "Probably not Georgie, but just about everything else."

"Matt, if I find you a coat hanger, will you give us a demonstration of dousing?" Kate asked him.

"Think not. Dousing's not a parlor trick." He softened the reprimand with a smile.

Kate tried for a quick recovery. "Oops, didn't mean to imply it was. Let me get you a drink. What's your pleasure?"

Matt sank into one of Kate's easy chairs as his wife Mary moved off to talk with Allison.

I pulled up a straight chair and sat down next to him. Here was a whole new idea for a display.

"Dousing. I'm not even sure I understand what that means," I said.

"City gal, I expect." He spoke in a slow, laconic manner that tickled me.

"You're right about that."

He leaned toward me, his brown eyes bright with enthusiasm.

"Dousing's an ancient art. Deals with searching for hidden things."

"In water?" I asked.

"Sometimes. Not always." A long pause.

I waited patiently. I'd learned how to talk with people in this part of the world. I knew not to rush them. I suspected Matt had more to say and I was right. After what seemed like an eternity by New York City standards, he cleared his throat.

"People associate dousing with finding water," he began. "I get calls to locate a septic tank, find the best spot to dig a well, projects like that. Folks think my rods tell me where there's water, but what I'm really picking up on is the energy of the water."

"Water has energy?"

"Damn tootin'. Everything does."

Kate came in from the kitchen and handed us each a beer. Matt took a long slow drink from his glass and wiped his hand across his mouth.

"But then how do you find things in the water itself?" I prompted him.

"I pick up energy from objects below the surface of the water, too. The pickup--that one I found last year--easy as falling out of a boat. My rods just about went crazy when we got over it. Damn fools had been fishing when they knew the ice was ripe to go. When they called me, they knew exactly where the truck went in, but we didn't find it anywhere near the place they said."

"Are you saying things move around down there?" I thought of the bateaux, slipping off into deep water, sometimes ending up a long way from where they were sunk. What had Don said? Sinking wasn't a precise art two hundred years ago. Apparently, it still wasn't.

"Yup. They move, move a lot. But there's a lot more to dousing than finding water and lost articles, you know." He paused again.

"Like..."

"Groundwater's one example. We should pay more attention so we wouldn't keep building over unhealthy spots the way we do."

"Groundwater? You mean ponds, swamps?"

"No, not surface water. Deeper down. Underground streams and rivers. They give off powerful energies, you know. Groundwater can cause cancer, other illness. People used to get dousers to tell them where to build. You put your house over an unhealthy site and you don't sleep right, wake up tired every day."

"I've had that happen," I said, surprised by a sudden rush of memory.

"And you blamed everything else, I'll wager. Never thought you were sleeping over a bad energy source."

He was right. I'd almost forgotten. I'd been thrilled when I rented my first New York apartment. I'd loved the place, but I'd slept poorly every night the entire time I lived there. I'd blamed problems at work, dissatisfaction with guys I dated, you name it. I knew from nothing about bad energy sources.

He smiled at my look of recognition.

"I'm right, aren't I? Look at Kate's dog over there. Dogs choose healthy places to sleep. Their instincts haven't gotten numbed by civilization like ours have. They pick safe places."

"So pets can tell you if you're getting bad energies?"

"Dogs can. Not cats, though. They like to sleep in places that are unhealthy for people. Part of their contrariness, I guess."

"Amazing," I said, spellbound.

"Ants are the worst of all. They love to build hills over places with high radiation."

"This is fascinating stuff. Could I watch you douse sometime, do you think?"

"Maybe. Depends."

I helped myself to a sheet of paper from Kate's telephone pad and wrote down my home and work numbers.

"Call me anytime. If you're dousing for anything at all, I'd love to watch. I promise I won't be any trouble."

As he folded the paper and put it into his shirt pocket, I was thinking about the recent happenings in our town--the murder of a beautiful young girl, the ugly rumors about her liaisons with local men, the financial difficulties facing some of our town's businesses. If only Matt could use his divining rods to uncover the bad energy sources causing our problems in Emerald Point--and find Tammy Stevenson's murderer in the process.

CHAPTER FIFTEEN

WHEN PAULINE ARRIVED at work Monday afternoon, she reached into her desk and handed me the minutes of the last community center committee meeting.

"Thought you might want to read these over before I make copies," she said.

"Thanks for the reminder. The meetings come on fast. I'd almost forgotten we scheduled it for this week." A large hunk of the mayor's time, I'd discovered, was devoted to meetings. Even more of it now with the summer season bearing down on us.

The committee masterminding the plan for a community center had been forging ahead on the project. Most of the members endorsed the idea except for a few dissenters who kept trying to peck the proposal to death just as they did with every other new idea that came along. To me, the more we kicked around plans for the center the better they sounded.

I glanced through the minutes. Perfect as always.

"Anything new on the murder investigation?" Pauline asked.

I shook my head.

"If there is, Jim hasn't seen fit to mention it to me," I said.

"Jim's a good man that way. Close-mouthed like his father. Those Thompson men have a lot of patience. They don't speak out until they're sure they know what they're talking about. Which is more than you can say for most folks around here."

"I'd appreciate a hint or two once in a while. That's all."

"It'll never happen. Might as well not get yourself shook up about it."

"So what have you heard, Pauline?"

"Well, you know the girl was a wild one. She ruffled more than a few feathers in her short life."

"But enough so somebody murdered her?"

"Happens. Ned used to say, 'If you want to get away with murder, this is the part of the world to do it in.' Don't know that things have changed much."

"What do you mean 'get away with murder'? Are you thinking they'll never find out who killed her?"

"Could happen, you know." Pauline picked up the minutes and took them to the copier. In five minutes she brought them back collated, stapled and ready to hand out at the meeting.

"Pauline, go home why don't you?," I said as I took them from her. "I want to do some work here anyway. There's no sense both of us hanging around."

"If it's okay with you..." She waited just long enough to make sure I wasn't going to change my mind, then gathered up her things and took off.

I was struggling with a report we had to file with the state when I heard someone in the outer office. Jack Roberts tapped on my door and came in.

"I see we've got that center committee meeting this week. You still want me to chair it?" he asked.

"Definitely. Pauline just finished copying the minutes from last time, if you want to see them."

Jack sat down in the chair in front of my desk and asked the question which had become part of every conversation this week: "Anything new on the murder investigation?"

I related Melissa's fears.

"She's afraid they'll never find out who killed Tammy."

"Wouldn't surprise me," Jack said.

"Why not? A girl gets murdered right here in our town and they may never find out who did it?"

"Found here, not necessarily murdered here. She hung out in the bars down in Lake George Village, maybe got involved with somebody she met there."

"Jim did tell me she was promiscuous. She worked in a half dozen motels around the lake, was linked to men in the places she worked."

"So they say." Jack's voice had an unexpected edge.

Suddenly something clicked.

"Wait a minute. Didn't she work at your place for a while?"

"Worked there one day. I'm hoping nobody will remember that. She left half way through her first day."

"Left?"

"Fired."

"Because..."

"If you want to know, give me a cup of that coffee." He pointed to the pot I'd started a few minutes before.

I poured us each a cup and sat back down.

"This has to be confidential. I'm sure you'll see why," he said.

I waited.

"Last spring, the housekeeper hired Tammy as a chambermaid, got her started her first day on the job, then left to go on an errand. A little while later the switchboard operator buzzed me and said Tammy needed somebody to come to the room she was cleaning. Said she sounded hysterical."

He took his time fixing his coffee, then drank more than half a cup before he went on.

"I swear those guys from security are never around when you need them. I rushed upstairs, third floor, a back bedroom we don't use much. The door was unlocked, so I went in. Tammy was lying on the bed, stretched out stark naked, not moving a muscle. I guess you could say she was artfully arranged, like those paintings they call odalisques. She could have been posing for *Playboy*. She was a beautiful girl, with a figure you wouldn't believe. I didn't know what to think."

I set down my coffee cup and gave him a disbelieving look.

"No, that's the truth. I'd never seen her before. I thought first I must have walked into the wrong room, embarrassed a guest. My second thought was that she'd been raped, except she looked very much at ease. I finally got the picture. She'd set up a tableau for my benefit. I was supposed to be so blown away I'd go along with what she was obviously suggesting."

"And did you?"

He reached over and pretended to cuff me on the side of the head.

"You have to ask? You don't give me much credit."

"To err is human."

"Loren, I'm trying to tell you something important here."

The expression on his face made me back off fast.

"Sorry. What did you do?"

"I told her to get dressed and get the hell out. I think everyone assumed she'd quit, so I didn't say any different."

"Did she collect her pay?"

61

He shoved his cup away and got to his feet.

"That's a funny thing to ask. I really don't know. We may have given her something. I wasn't anxious for the story to get out. Do you have any idea the ribbing I'd have taken over there?"

"Really?"

"You bet, really." He grabbed for the minutes. His hands were shaking.

Okay, so I hadn't made the right responses. How could I when I still wasn't sure what they should have been?

He rustled the papers several times as if he was skimming through them, then gave up the pretense.

"I'll take these with me to look over," he said.

I walked out of the office with him, casting around for something to say. Todd Lewis was sitting in the reception area. He appeared to be engrossed in a magazine, too engrossed. I wondered if he'd overheard our conversation.

"Todd, hi," I said.

Jack ignored him and banged out the door.

Todd stood up and shifted awkwardly from one foot to the other.

"My mother told me you telephoned and asked how I was. She got a kick out of it."

"Come on in. What can I do for you?" I led him into my office. I waited for him to tell me why he was there. Nothing. He'd managed his opening remarks, then run out of steam.

"They're sayin' Tammy was murdered," he blurted out finally.

"I heard that, too. Go on."

"I've got something of hers I want to send you. You figure out what to do with it. I'm outta here."

"What do you mean?"

"Gettin' the hell out of Dodge, my dad would say."

"I don't understand."

"You will when you see what I'm sending you. The only thing is you can't do anything with it for a couple days. Give me a chance to get clear of this place."

"Todd, I really don't understand. Are you in some kind of trouble?"

He stared at me with a look I couldn't read. Maybe he was still in pain from his fall, but what I was seeing in his face didn't look like physical pain. He was hiding something. Before I could ask another question, he jumped to his feet and bolted out of the office.

Maybe Jim was right. Maybe Todd Lewis knew more about Tammy's murder than I'd thought.

Chapter Sixteen

The committee planning our new community center had scheduled a meeting for four o'clock Friday afternoon. Shortly before noon, as I was setting up the conference room, the phone rang.

"Jack wants to reschedule the meeting," Margaret Collins, Jack's secretary said. "He'd like to make it five o'clock over here at the Emerald Point Inn. He's expecting an important phone call and can't take a chance on missing it."

"Something wrong with his cell phone?" I snapped, then apologized. "Sorry, Marge. I didn't mean to shoot the messenger. I'll be there."

By five o'clock, Margaret, the personification of the efficient secretary, had managed to get word to everyone. What she couldn't do was keep the committee members from gathering in the bar before the meeting began. Not a good idea for this crowd, especially on a Friday afternoon. One thing led to another--as they so often do in bars--and by the time the group adjourned to the inn's large meeting room, most of the members had downed at least one drink and possibly more.

As people straggled in and sat down, I mentally checked off their names. Most of the Inn Crowd were taking part since they saw the value of anything which brought tourists to Emerald Point. Peter and Jane Finch sat across from me next to Ramona and Deke Dolley. Arthur Clark, owner of a motel a few miles north of us, joined them and several members of the town council squeezed in at the end of the table.

I was surprised when Jack welcomed Don Morrison, his hair still wet from an afternoon of diving, and Stephanie Colvin from the *Post Standard*. Neither had been on the committee before. Jack had apparently taken it on himself to add new members.

BENEATH THE SURFACE

We were about to start the meeting when the door to the conference room swung open and Tom Bailey, red-faced and bumbling, slid into the chair next to me. He yanked his tie away from his loosened collar and set a full bottle of beer--obviously not his first—on the table in front of him. He looked sloppy and unkempt, very different from the neat guy in sport clothes I'd seen emerge from Melissa Taggert's kitchen the day I'd called on her.

"That was nice of you to stop over to see Mel," he muttered under his breath. "She 'preciated it."

I shrugged. Jack was trying to quiet the group.

"Bob wanted me to help him move some stuff before his relatives got there. Clean up the place a little. I didn't know he'd decided to go into work."

"You told me," I whispered

"Bob's got a mess out in that garage. Lot of it is too big for one person to move."

I nodded. Something was going on here. When Tom appeared in the Taggert's living room, I hadn't sensed anything strange about his presence at the house. Now I wondered why he was trying so hard to explain it.

Jack eventually brought the meeting to order and Marge, acting as secretary, read through the minutes Pauline had typed. The month before, Jack had offered an unused building on the inn's grounds as a site for the community center. The next step would be deciding what aspects of the lake and its history we should include in our displays.

"Major Robert Rogers," Reggie Collins, Pauline's husband, intoned as he got to his feet to introduce his all-time favorite topic. I groaned inwardly when he launched into his spiel about Rogers' Rangers and their role in the French and Indian War. Reggie, a dedicated re-enactor, often dressed in colonial costume to depict Rogers at local events. I enjoyed his portrayal of the Major, admired his knowledge of Colonial history, but enough already. Today we had too much else on the agenda.

Reggie stopped short, almost as if he'd read my thoughts.

"Well, you all know about Rogers' Rock and the Rangers' exploits on the lake. Every kid around here has heard the story of the Battle on Snowshoes. I can see us with a diorama showing that scene easy enough, but now there's something new."

George Tyler, always the spoilsport, interrupted Reggie's dramatic pause.

"I'll tell you what's new, Reggie, and it's time you faced up to it. That business about them puttin' their snowshoes on backwards and makin' the tracks look like they went off the cliff is a myth. Everybody admits that now."

Reggie looked stricken, but he pressed on.

"Let me finish what I was going to say, George. They think they might have found Rogers' remains over in New Hampshire, that he came back here from England and died near his relatives over there."

"No way. Couldn't be," George snorted.

"Could so," Reggie shot back.

I waited for Jack to intervene, but he said nothing. He stared past Reggie, obviously a million miles away, making no attempt to take charge. I leaned forward and spoke in my most assertive manner.

"Wait a minute, George. Why don't we let Reggie fill us in on the details first."

Reggie smiled a bit too smugly but, surprisingly, George let him get away with it.

"Rogers had gone back to England a broken man," Reggie continued. "Understand--this was the hero who'd fired the imagination of the colonists and defined the rules of wilderness fighting. But, at that point, his wife had divorced him, he was drinking heavily, even got sent to debtors' prison. A brilliant career come to an ignominious end. Even hard core disbelievers can see the tragedy of that." He glared at George.

George sniffed and opened his mouth to interrupt. I reached over and tapped the table in front of him, signaling him to wait.

"So," Reggie said, "folks have found a cemetery over in New Hampshire where they think Rogers might be buried. Want to douse to check for his DNA, but they can't get permission to do it."

"Can you actually douse for somebody's DNA?" I blurted out, but Reggie was too preoccupied to hear me. Where was Matt the douser when I needed him?

"What I want to do is introduce some of these new findings at the Third of July Festival. I'm willing to build a booth to display my Rogers memorabilia. In fact, some of us could probably man the booth in our Ranger uniforms, if folks wanted us to."

Several people at the table ducked their heads, trying to conceal their smiles. It was no secret how much Reggie loved dressing in his colonial garb.

He pretended not to notice the smiles.

"Might be a good way to introduce folks to the center concept, I say."

"Hey Reggie, if you do that, then why can't Bateaux Below do a booth too?" Don Morrison said. "We can display diving gear and hand out material on zebra mussels and the annual cleanup."

Blank looks from most of the committee. The early cocktail hour was taking its toll.

At least one person was paying attention. Stephanie Colvin looked up from taking notes for her article.

"You both may be on to something," she said. "This isn't a bad idea at all--using your Third of July Festival to publicize plans for the center. Maybe there could be other displays, too."

As George grumbled ineffectually, several members woke up enough to agree that the idea might have merit. Definitely a tide-turning moment. Jack, lost far out at sea, didn't react.

The Third of July Festival, like almost everything else Emerald Point did, had always struck me as a day late and a dollar short--except technically with this event we were a day early. Other towns had nailed down the Fourth with super fireworks, hot air balloons and special events. So far, all Emerald Point had come up with was this village-wide craft festival. A preview of some of the exhibits planned for our community center would definitely be a step up. Why didn't Jack grab the idea and run with it?

Reggie had launched into an explanation of the problems of dousing for DNA when the inn's switchboard operator tiptoed across the room and whispered something in Jack's ear.

"Excuse me. I've got to take this call." Jack raced for the door without bothering to ask anyone to take over his chairman duties.

The meeting fell apart. Reggie couldn't get out another complete sentence; the council members looked appalled; the Inn Crowd started buzzing among themselves about their favorite topic--the shortage of summer employees. Tom Bailey took the last swig from his beer bottle and headed for the bar. Several others at the table seconded his motion and followed suit. In less than a minute, we'd passed the point of no return.

As we filed out of the conference room, Don moved in close behind me.

"Have a drink with me," he said.

"I could sure use one," I told him as I mentally catalogued the grievances I'd present to Jack the next time I saw him.

"Damn it, maybe I should have taken over the meeting, but I can't make every community project my personal responsibility. Things never work out that way," I said.

"Makes sense to me," he said.

"Where are we going?" I asked when I realized we'd bypassed the Inn's bar and walked into the lobby.

"Any place but here," Don said. "I've had enough nonsense for one day, haven't you? I've been wanting to check out the Beach House on the Point. Let's take a ride over there."

He was right. I'd had enough nonsense not just for one day, but for the entire summer. Let Jack clean up his own mess. Without further discussion, I accompanied Don to his car. No warning bells went off in my head, or if they did, I was too angry to hear them.

CHAPTER SEVENTEEN

THE BEACH HOUSE on the Point boasted one of the best locations on the lake, but the rambling, three-story building was badly rundown. Phil Johnson, the third generation in the Johnson family to own the inn, lacked the capital to redecorate but found ways to disguise his establishment's shortcomings. Soft lighting and efficient service soothed his patrons into thinking they were in a much more elegant place.

"I don't know about you, but I'm starving," Don said as he steered me toward the terrace. "I just remembered I forgot all about lunch. Do you mind if we have our drinks out here and get something to eat?"

"Not if we go Dutch," I said.

"I'd like to argue that point, but I suspect I'd lose," he said with a smile.

Against a stunning background of lake and sky, the dimly lighted terrace was set for formal dining. The tables were covered with white linen tablecloths and adorned with flowers and fat candles under sparkling chimneys. Most of the diners were couples talking quietly, concerned only with each other. Honeymooners, I suspected. It was the season for that after all, and Phil offered a special package each year to attract this particular clientele.

Don spoke a few quiet words to the hostess and we were escorted to a table next to the low stone parapet on the outer edge of the covered terrace. From my seat I looked across the rolling green lawn at a magnificent vista. Here on the point, the lake stretched away from us in three directions. The dark water shimmered under a full moon with one wide swath of florescence strung across it like a silver band.

After he'd asked my preference in wines, Don ordered a bottle of Merlot and insisted we share an assortment of Beach House appetizers--jumbo shrimp, crab and lobster Phil had brought in from Maine on overnight runs.

The night was perfect--warmer weather at last--and the big overhead fans swirled the air lazily above us. Don wisely steered the conversation away from the meeting and its unfortunate conclusion. He asked instead about my reasons for moving to the lake.

"I visited here every summer as a child," I told him. "When my grandfather died and left me the house, I came here to sell it. I was getting over a divorce, and the lake always seemed to have healing powers for me. Eventually, I decided I belonged here."

"And you got yourself elected mayor. How did you manage that?" He refilled our wineglasses, which somehow had emptied quickly.

"I found myself involved in some of the local squabbles, most of them concerned with an infestation of milfoil in the cove near my grandfather's property, and I wanted to see what could be done about it. I began going to meetings and the next thing I knew I was immersed in politics," I said.

He leaned forward, totally focused on what I was saying.

"But being accepted so quickly in a small town and elected to office--that's unusual," he said.

"I was surprised, myself. People remembered me from all the times I came here to visit my grandparents as a child, so I wasn't a complete stranger. And it helped that I didn't belong to any particular faction."

"That's not exactly the way I've heard it. I've been told you dazzled everyone--smart, articulate and beautiful, besides. Not a bad combination."

"Who have you been talking to?" I dismissed the compliment quickly, uncomfortable with flattery even when it seemed sincere.

Don took a different tack.

"Had you been political before in New York?"

"A little. A congressman's campaign, neighborhood matters. I knew something about codes and ordinances. That helped."

The waiter brought our dinners--beautifully presented as my friend Kate the caterer would have said--a pasta with vegetables for me, and a broiled fish plate for Don. As we ate, I took over the questioning.

"I was a college professor in Albany," Don said. "Living on the lake was my goal for a long time. Now that I've reached it, I'm content to do just enough to keep the wolf from the door. I act as consultant for several companies and I can always teach a course or two if I want."

So we were both starting new lives. Interesting. But then, others in Emerald Point had done the same thing. We were the new immigrants to the region, the *flatlanders*--as people further north in the Adirondacks called outsiders who moved in.

"What kind of companies?" I asked, but Don didn't get a chance to answer.

Phil Johnson, swaying slightly on the balls of his feet, approached our table. He checked out our almost empty plates.

"Everything satisfactory, Mayor? I sure hope you liked your dinner, seeing as how you're slummin' tonight."

I let the remark hang in the air for a minute. I hated cracks like that, the implication that I was a snob, that I didn't frequent his place often enough. Snide comments were an occupational hazard in my job; I got pelted with them more often than I liked.

"Why would you say something like that, Phil?" I went on the offensive, though less aggressively than I would have done in my New York days. "You've got no call to run down your own place like that. My meal was delicious. Did you think it wouldn't be?"

Phil responded with a flustered look. I jumped up, scraping my chair along the stone terrace.

"Don, you promised to take me for a walk outside. Maybe we can come back later for our coffee," I urged.

Don caught on immediately. He was on his feet in an instant.

"You're right. I did promise, didn't I? I think that's the *Saint* coming up the lake, so this is a perfect time for a walk."

We descended the low steps leading to the lawn. I could see Phil shaking his head in bewilderment at our sudden departure. Being a public servant might mean I had to temper my comments even to guys like Phil who deserved a put down, but I didn't have to sit still for their cracks.

"Thanks for the fast pick-up," I said to Don as we headed toward the lake. "If I'd stayed, I probably would have said something I'd regret later. My New York friends wouldn't believe the new kinder, gentler me."

"Kinder, gentler?" he said, raising his eyebrows.

From the table where we'd been sitting, we'd seen the *Lac du Saint Sacrement*, the largest of the lake steamers, skirting the opposite shore of the lake. Now, it made a wide swing and came directly toward us as it prepared to turn south and head back toward Lake

George Village. The huge white ship, ablaze with lights, looked like a confection worthy of a royal wedding.

"What do you do with yourself when you're not working at being mayor?" He said when we sat down on a bench near the dock. He leaned close to me. I felt his arm brush against mine as he pointed to the couples on the *Lac* who were waving at us from the upper deck. I smelled the fresh, pleasing scent of his shampoo. A few days ago I'd pegged him as too hairy for my taste, but tonight with his blond hair and beard accented by moonlight, he could have posed for the cover of a romance novel.

What was the question again--*what did I do with myself?*

"I have quite a few evening meetings, so some nights it just seems good to be free. And I have friends here. I get together with them occasionally," I said.

"Does that sometimes include male friends, single male friends, that is?"

I was framing a careful reply when Phil Johnson lurched down the lawn and planted himself in front of us.

Phil scrunched up his face to show his confusion.

"Did I say something out of line back there, Mayor? Sorry if I offended you in some way. Especially since I've got a favor to ask you. Walk over here with me, will ya?" He pointed toward the campground just beyond the Beach House lawn.

"To the campground, you mean?" I really didn't owe Phil any favors, but maybe I'd been too sharp. I got to my feet and followed him across the lawn. Don hesitated. After a few seconds, he stood up and followed us.

I'd made a point, when I was elected mayor, of familiarizing myself with the makeup of the Point. The Beach House occupied prime location on the southern edge. The section north of it, beyond a screen of trees, was filled with trailers, close packed, four or five rows of them stretching from the highway down an easy slope to the water. The trailers were set parallel to the lakeshore, just far enough apart to accommodate a tarp or canopy. Their owners used these makeshift patios for eating, socializing and--sometimes on the hottest nights--sleeping outdoors. Farther north, out of our line of vision, the campground was divided into fifty or sixty campsites, usually by this time of year a small village of tents and campers.

"Are they full over there already?" I asked Phil.

"Why wouldn't they be? This here's the best spot on the lake and it costs practically nothing to rent a site. It's not fair to those of us running a business and paying big taxes that we have to put up with this kind of competition."

"Bring that up at a council meeting, Phil. Get some facts together and we can put you on the agenda whenever you want."

"Hurts my business to have this campground here. I've tried to tell people that, but Jeannie Spenser is the only one seems to listen."

Had Phil been talking to Jeannie about selling the Beach House? Gossip about Phil's financial troubles made the rounds periodically. Since Jeannie brokered most of the important real estate deals on the lake, she'd be the logical choice if Phil wanted to sell.

Phil pressed on, determined to make his point.

"Seems obvious the campground's the problem. They have half dozen fights over there every week. One night the deputies had to come back twice. Something like that drives my business away, I'm saying."

"Phil, telling me about this isn't good enough. Check with the sheriff's department, make sure they're taking your complaints seriously. Then, you're going to have to come to a council meeting and bring this out in the open," I said.

"Drives business away, I'm telling you. Why just last week..."

As Phil geared up to prolong the discussion, I turned to Don.

"We'd better get going, hadn't we? Looks like they're ready to close the terrace for the night."

Don took my arm and we hurried across the lawn to settle our bill with our waitress.

"Sorry if we held you up," I told her, adding another five dollars to our already adequate tip. I'd waited tables myself. I knew from experience how those final hours dragged when the hangers-on couldn't tear themselves away.

"Is it like that for you all the time? Don't you go any place without running into people with problems?" Don asked as he drove me back to the Inn parking lot to pick up my car.

"Oh sure, once in a while," I said casually. But I could sense the evening's mood had soured. There had been no more questions about my having single male friends, no talk of getting together another time.

My white Saab stood all by itself in an empty section of the Inn's parking lot. Don dropped me off and waited for me to pull out onto the highway. Then he drove off in the opposite direction.

Chapter Eighteen

AT SIX O'CLOCK the next morning, the sunlight streaming through my bedroom windows brought me back to life, or to an approximation of it, anyway. No, I protested, I can't be waking up this early on my day off. My head was complaining the way a head does when its owner has poured too much wine into it. I burrowed deep into the covers for ten minutes and then gave up. Coffee. Maybe that would help.

As soon as I'd forced down my requisite two cups, I grabbed a bathing suit out of the closet and slipped into it. The air felt comfortable as I walked down to the dock, but I wasn't deceived. Lake George was spring fed and that meant cold, even on a pleasant June day. I didn't dare dive in--that move could have brought on an instant heart attack--and the slow wade along the dock was pure torture. I finally numbed up enough to swim back and forth parallel to the shore. After a few minutes my head felt better, but perhaps it had just turned as numb as my extremities.

I thought I heard a voice, but I was slow to realize someone was calling my name. I lifted my face out of the water and saw Kate Donohue standing halfway between the house and the dock.

"Loren, you're moving. You must be alive. Can't you hear me?"

"Now I can. You're out early," I said.

"Is there coffee? Can I get myself a cup?"

"Sure, if you bring one for me, too." I could see a white paper bag under Kate's arm, bulging with what looked suspiciously like breakfast treats.

I climbed out on the dock and grabbed a towel. Fortunately, I'd brought one large enough to wrap up in and heavy enough to keep me from freezing to death. I settled into one of the wooden Adirondack chairs I'd arranged under the trees in the front yard.

In a few minutes, Kate joined me carrying a tray with two mugs of coffee and a plate of her special raspberry Danish. She sat down next to me and laid blue checked napkins on the broad wooden arms of our chairs with her best catering flourish.

I sipped the hot coffee gratefully as I unwrapped my Danish. "Glad to see you. And your Danish, too. Nice surprise," I said.

"Hardly a surprise. You knew I'd be dying to find out what you've been up to."

"What I've been up to?"

"Must have been something really bad if you felt the need of symbolic cleansing. That water has to be mighty cold."

"Symbolic cleansing? You're right. The water is cold and it has apparently numbed my brain along with everything else. I don't take your meaning."

"Of course, that's it. You're numbing yourself so you don't have to feel guilt. That's the reason you were thrashing around like a madwoman out in that lake, isn't it?" Kate studied my face like Investigator Thompson trying to extract a confession, but I caught the twitching in the corners of her mouth as she fought back a smile.

"Oh I get it. You're talking about Don. You already know I went to dinner with him."

"As does most of the town. The news has pushed speculation about the murder right off the front page."

I shook my head. A serious mistake, it turned out. Even though my hangover had loosened its stranglehold, shaking my head was still off limits. "I'll never get used to this place. What's that ad? Traveling at the speed of business? They should change it to traveling at the speed of Emerald Point gossip."

"And your outing with Don makes for particularly juicy gossip, fit for the tabloids. Lovely young mayor involved in secret rendezvous with outsider. But, don't let me jump to conclusions too quickly. Tell me everything and I'll help you decide on the proper spin."

"Kate, I hate to disappoint you, but we had a casual dinner, nothing more."

She made a face. "Damn. Are you sure you just aren't telling?"

"I swear there's nothing to tell. We were about to have our coffee when Phil Johnson butted in and dragged me over to the trailer park. Typical Phil. He's annoyed the park's there, but he's too lazy to get his act together and file a formal complaint. Instead, he insisted I peek over the fence and check the place out."

"I heard they'd been having trouble up there. Did he want you to be an eyewitness to something?" Kate asked.

"If he did, he was disappointed. The park was quiet as could be. He spoiled our dinner for nothing."

"An unromantic turn of events."

"You've got that right. Your average guy doesn't cotton to a woman being called into action as a public official part way through a pleasant evening," I said.

"But it was a pleasant evening then, at least until Phil wrecked it?"

"I'd have to say so. Actually, Don is a pretty interesting guy to spend time with, which--and I'd like to make this perfectly clear, Your Honor--was all I was doing."

"So you and Don took off right after the meeting. I heard it ground to a halt. Was that Jack's fault?"

"Ground to a halt is too kind a description. Jack wasn't handling things very well anyway, then was called away for a phone call. He bolted out the door without asking anyone to take over. Several of our illustrious members seized the opportunity to rush the bar."

"And then…"

"Kate, I'm freezing. Let's go inside and get a refill."

"Sure, just when we hit the good part." Kate pretended dismay, but she got to her feet and gathered up the mugs and napkins. "Don't think you've diverted me, because you haven't," she warned as we climbed the slate steps to the house.

"Give me one minute to get some clothes on," I said as I disappeared into the downstairs bathroom.

"Keep talking," Kate called to me through the half-open door. "I expect Jack will arrive momentarily to explain why he messed up the meeting. By the way, there's a package on your side porch. Want me to get it?"

"No, that's all right. Probably Pauline dropped something off. I'm not sure you're right about Jack. He's got other things on his mind."

"How did you happen to leave with Don? I think you skipped over that part," Kate asked, as I returned in the jeans and tee shirt I had left hanging in the bathroom.

"Don asked if I wanted to get a drink. I agreed, thinking he meant to go into the bar at the Inn. The next thing I knew we were leaving and I didn't care. I wanted out of there. Now, are you satisfied?"

"Not really. I would have preferred pulsating passion, a breathless dash to his car, the forbidden rendezvous I mentioned earlier."

"You've been reading those romance novels again, haven't you? All right. Our eyes met; we were overwhelmed with passion, panting with anticipation. We couldn't wait to get away so we could ravish each other and..." I stopped in mid-sentence as Kate's face registered not the amusement I expected, but embarrassment. I turned around. Jack had come in the back door and was standing behind me.

"See what happens when people don't knock?" I felt my face burn, but I held my head high and bluffed it out. I squeezed one last cup of coffee from the carafe and handed it to Jack as I pointed to an empty chair at the table.

Kate bounced out of her chair and dashed for the door. "Well, my work here is done. There's one more Danish left. You guys can fight over it if you run out of other things to argue about."

I started to follow her out. I would have liked to leave myself, but it was my house. "So," I said to Jack as I sat back down.

"Girl talk. I'm always surprised at how explicit it can be."

"You know we were joking, don't you?" I'd give him that much.

Jack stared at me without speaking. I couldn't guess at what was coming--an angry outburst, an apology for the meeting, an explanation about the phone call. His face was a mask, his feelings hidden deep behind it.

Finally, he said, "Loren, something is terribly wrong."

I waited. He didn't seem to know how to continue. I prompted him. "Wrong?"

"My father. My father's mucked up bad. Real bad. The call at the meeting yesterday came from the bank. I should have made him put my name on the business years ago, but he kept saying he'd take care of it and I hated to force the issue. I've tried to discuss things with him so many times. He's been trying to cook up some deal with Jeannie Spenser, I guess, but he won't tell me about it. Now we could lose everything."

I took a deep breath as I tried to switch gears. Jack hadn't been thinking about me or the meeting or where I'd gone afterward. He had bigger problems to worry about. "Lose everything? It can't be that bad, can it?"

"Damn it. It certainly can be. Take my word for it. He's spent a ton of money in the last year and it hasn't all gone into the hotel."

"Where has it gone?"

"That's the hell of it. I don't know. He drinks, I know that. But I don't see how even heavy drinking could siphon off that much. Anyway, I think he does most of his drinking at the hotel or in his own apartment. Gambling, maybe. But I don't see any sign that he does much of that. I don't know what to think, except that we're close to bankruptcy and I have no idea why."

"Jack, I'm so sorry."

"So you picked a piss poor time to teach me a lesson, if that's what you were doing, letting the meeting fall apart like that."

His remark stung like a slap. I gasped, shocked by the change in his tone, by the harshness of his voice.

"Excuse me? You expected me to take over and get the meeting back on track after you made a shambles of it?"

"Damn it all, Loren." His voice was a stranger's voice.

"Hang on." I stopped him before he could say more. "Let's not do this. This isn't the time for an argument about the meeting. Tell me more about what's wrong."

"Loren," he said again, but whatever he planned to add was interrupted by loud knocking at the back door. My day for unexpected visitors.

The inside door was open. I could see a uniformed figure through the screen. Rick Cronin stood there, his big fist raised to knock again. "Mayor Graham," he said as I approached him. "Investigator Thompson sent me to pick you up. He wants you to come with me right away."

A million thoughts crowded into my mind. Kate, first. An accident on the way home? No, it would be too soon to hear something like that. Besides, I'd resolved to stop pushing the panic button every time I got called into action. In a small town the mayor could be wanted for any number of reasons, not all of them very serious. Maybe this was something as silly as the rattlesnake incident.

"Give me a minute to change into something more presentable," I said.

"No. He says you gotta come right now. Emergency."

So it wasn't a joke.

Jack didn't ask what was wrong or if he could do anything to help. He bolted past Rick and out of the back door.

I didn't waste time, either. I grabbed the package off the side porch, tossed it onto the kitchen counter and followed Rick out.

CHAPTER NINETEEN

RICK OPENED THE front door of his patrol car and motioned me to get in. His ruddy, twenty-five year old face was set in an unfamiliar scowl as he swung out of my driveway and zigzagged through the Emerald Point streets. I tensed, expecting him to start blaring his siren.

"Rick, where are we going?" I asked him.

"Sorry, Ms. Graham. Orders from the boss. We'll be there in a minute, anyway." He turned onto the highway and headed north.

A few minutes later he pulled into Deke and Ramona's motel. Two other sheriff's vehicles and an ambulance were parked in front of the cabin next to the Dolley's combination home and office.

"Oh no. What's happened here?" I asked.

"He wants to talk to you himself," Rick said. He tapped out two short blasts on his horn.

At what was obviously a prearranged signal, Jim emerged from the first cabin and loped over to us. I opened the door and got out.

"I figured you'd want to know about this, Mayor, but you're not going to like it."

"What's happened?" This was certainly a day for bad news.

"Deke's been shot. Maybe did it himself, maybe not. They're trying to stabilize him enough to move him to the hospital. You don't want to see him, but Ramona could use a woman friend right now," Jim said.

"How bad is he hurt?" I asked.

"Looks pretty bad to me, but it will be up to the doctors to make that call."

I glanced down the row of cabins. I hadn't realized the Dolley's motel was in such bad shape. From the highway the brown log walls looked rustic, but up close, they were pathetically shabby and worn. The little porches sagged; most of the gray deck paint had been worn clear through. Metal chairs, their once cheerful red finish pockmarked by rusty gouges, were ready for a trip to the landfill. Who would stay here? Certainly not a vacationing family. The place invited only vagrants, the dispossessed, the desperately poor.

Ramona was crumpled in one of the chairs on the front porch of the cabin Jim had come from. I hesitated, not sure what I was supposed to do.

"Go to her, why don't you," Jim said. "But better not look inside. It's bad in there. You don't want to see it."

"Ramona," I called as I ran up the steps toward her. She stared up at me with no sign of recognition. "Ramona, it's Loren."

I reached out to her and pulled her against me in an awkward hug. She didn't try to stand or move away, just huddled in the chair, her face swollen and streaked with tears. She appeared spent, her usually perky manner replaced by a look of utter dejection.

I knelt down next to her. "Ramona, what happened here? Can you tell me?"

"A robber. Do you believe it, a robber? Like we had something to steal. He wanted money. Money. We haven't had a piece of meat in weeks. The people at the church give us cheese and vegetables. I told Deke I should ask for some hamburger or something but he didn't want me to say anything."

Jim and I exchanged glances, both of us shocked at how close to the breaking point she was.

"Oh, Ramona, did you tell anyone how bad things were for you? People would have helped," I said.

She lifted her chin, straightened ever so slightly in the chair.

"We still had our pride, Loren. I couldn't go around telling how bad off we were. We thought about selling, but we waited too long to make up our minds, I guess. We kept thinking if we just had a good season, we could fix the place up a little and then we could sell it."

I patted her arm, as I tried to decide what to do next. Jim and Rick had disappeared into the cabin. I could hear their voices discussing Deke's condition.

When Jim poked his head out the door, I stood up.

"Why don't I take Ramona over to the house, maybe make some coffee or something?" I asked him.

"Good idea. We've notified her daughter. She'll be here as soon as she can." Jim wrapped an arm around Ramona and, supporting most of her weight, guided her toward the house. He pushed open the back door and eased her toward a chair at the kitchen table.

I followed close behind them. Once inside, I glanced around, appalled at the condition of Ramona's kitchen. I saw no sign of a coffee maker, just stacks of dirty dishes cluttering the sink and overflowing onto the counter next to it. The floor was grimy with dirt. The half-open drawers in the cupboards disgorged stained towels, papers and an appalling collection of junk. Something had been terribly wrong here. Both Ramona and Deke always appeared neat and well put together when I saw them out in public. Apparently, neither of them had done any cleaning in a long time.

I emptied the sink and drew water, thinking I would at least make a stab at washing the dirty dishes, but the water ran cold as ice. I filled the tea kettle and set it on one of the burners of the gas stove, then located an old-fashioned percolator and started coffee. Ramona slumped in the chair. Her low-pitched keening made me feel like crying along with her.

Jim disappeared for a few minutes, then returned and pulled up a chair across from her.

"You've got to tell me what happened, Ramona, and you've got to tell me straight. I don't see any signs of robbery. What made you think someone was trying to rob Deke?"

"Yes, somebody was robbing him. I saw him."

"You saw the person. What did he look like?"

"I don't know. I was scared. I didn't look at him close."

"And why was Deke in that cabin? Is that where the robber was?"

"Yes. No." She shook her head rapidly from side to side. "I don't know. I don't know. Leave me be."

Jim continued the questioning, his voice gentle, but insistent.

"Ramona, you've got to tell me the truth. Did you really see a robber?"

Instead of answering him, Ramona resumed the low, humming noise deep in her throat. Her gray hair, already untidy, came loose from the pins holding it and fell forward around her face.

"Listen to me, Ramona. Do you think Deke shot himself? You might as well tell me. What's the sense trying to hide it?" Jim said.

Before Ramona could reply, the back door swung open and her daughter Jeannie Spenser rushed into the room. Saturday was obviously not a day off for Jeannie, unless she dressed exceptionally well to lounge around the house. Her elegant navy business suit and matching high heels shouted exclusive New York designer labels. Her platinum hair had been colored and styled to perfection, her makeup, artfully applied. Ramona and I stared at her like women in a Walker Evans photograph.

"Mother, what in the world has happened? Are you all right?" she asked.

Ramona reached out her arms and drew the younger woman to her. "Jeannie, Deke's shot. He's out there in the first cabin with blood all over him."

Jeannie disentangled herself and turned to Jim. "I'm Jeannie Spencer, Ramona's daughter. Is that true--Deke's been shot?"

"I'm afraid it is. Ma'am, I'm trying to find out just how it happened. Maybe your mother will feel more comfortable talking about it now that you're here," Jim said.

Jeannie pulled up a chair next to Ramona and sat down. She held herself stiffly, making no move to touch her mother. She listened carefully but didn't intervene as Jim pounded away with his questioning.

When the tea kettle began to boil, I emptied it into the sink and added a generous splash of the dish detergent I'd dug out of the cupboard. I washed and rinsed four coffee cups, and as soon as the coffee finished perking, I poured us each a cup. Glad to be occupied, I kept mine with me at the sink while I filled the kettle again and continued washing dishes. I heard the refrain of questions and answers repeated over and over until I was ready to beg Jim to stop. Finally, Ramona broke down.

"Yes, all right. He tried to kill himself, if that's what you want to hear. He went out to the cabin early this morning. I didn't know what he was doing out there. Then I heard the shot and rushed out and he was lying there."

"Ramona, I'm sorry," Jim said.

Jeannie remained surprisingly quiet. I recalled hearing that she'd opposed her mother's marriage to Deke. "Had he bought life insurance recently, Mother? Were you afraid he wouldn't be covered if he killed himself?" she asked in a matter-of-fact way.

Ramona nodded, fresh tears streaming down her cheeks.

Jeannie didn't acknowledge her mother's tears. Her face remained set in the same uncompromising expression. "That happened to family friends of ours," she told Jim. "They couldn't collect because the man had just taken out the policy and there was a waiting period for suicide. It would be just like Deke to make that same mistake."

Ramona flinched at the cruelty of the remark. "Oh, Jeannie, how can you say something like that now?" she said.

"Jim," someone called from outside.

Through the screen I could see members of the rescue squad easing a stretcher into the ambulance. I assumed the form swathed in blankets was Deke, but I couldn't tell if he was alive or dead.

Jim moved quickly to the door. "Ms. Spenser, you and your mother will probably want to head down to the hospital. I can have a deputy drive you. I have a few more questions, but they can wait until later."

"It's not necessary to have someone drive us. I'll bring my mother in my car," Jeannie said, taking control. She turned to me. "Thanks for helping. If you'll just finish up the dishes and make sure the stove and lights are turned off. Then, before you leave, be sure both front and back doors are locked. We'll go along."

Jeannie's name might be soft and feminine, but her manner was anything but. Her no-holds-barred real estate business in Lake George Village was the scourge of the smaller agencies all around the lake. As she'd just demonstrated, her management style was direct, tougher than that of some Manhattan CEO's I'd met. I sometimes wondered if it would catch up with her eventually, but what did I know? Local gossip claimed her business grew every year.

Once outside, Ramona pulled herself together enough to ask about riding in the ambulance with Deke. When Jim turned thumbs down on the idea, Jeannie guided her mother to her black Volvo and they took off at top speed following the ambulance.

I took my instructions seriously, not because Jeannie Spenser expected me to, but because I wanted to do anything I could to help Ramona. With one more kettle of hot water, I finished washing the dishes and left them in the drainer. Then I walked through the house to check the front door. In marked contrast to the kitchen, the other rooms were in perfect order. Official-looking documents, not jumbled in untidy clutter like the papers in the kitchen but stacked in neat piles, covered the dining room table. Next to an open metal strong box, I saw a sheaf of papers with the word *Mortgage* in large letters. Beside it, were piles of what appeared to be bills, the words *past due* stamped in red letters across the ones on top. I knew not to touch anything. The explanation for Deke's suicide attempt would probably be found right here on this table.

As I always did when I visited Ramona, I stopped to admire her antique cherry buffet, a magnificent piece of furniture with a rich patina and beautifully carved legs. Ramona wisely kept it free of clutter, using only slim silver candlesticks with beeswax candles, one on each end. "If you ever decide to sell it..." I sometimes said, but I knew she'd never part with it.

As I went out the back door, I saw Jim emerging from the cabin with Rick Cronin in tow. "I assume you've seen the papers on the dining room table?" I said.

"You didn't touch anything, did you?"

I fell back on Josie's classic response. I rolled my eyes at him in disgust.

Jim took my arm and escorted me to Rick Cronin's car as if he couldn't get rid of me fast enough.

"Is there something happening here I'm not picking up on?" I asked him.

"We aren't jumping to any conclusions here, Mayor. This may be a tough one. If Deke dies, that'll make two bodies this month and that's N.G. for your little town. You want me to proceed with caution, don't you?"

"Are you thinking now Deke didn't try to commit suicide? You seemed so determined to get Ramona to agree that he did."

"Don't go reading too much into anything. We'll take this one step by step. I'll be in touch." He shoved the car door shut and signaled to Rick to take off.

On the ride home I ran a few questions by Rick, but he remained as closemouthed as he'd been on our trip to the motel. When he dropped me off at my house, I didn't even go inside. Instead, I got into my own car and headed for Kate Donohue's. I hadn't connected very well with the men around here during the last twenty-four hours. With Kate, things would be different. I could count on her to dish out moral support as generously as she served up her gourmet meals.

At least I could have counted on her if she'd been home. She wasn't. Even Josie might have offered a sympathetic word, but it would have been unreasonable to expect her to be around on a Saturday afternoon.

I had no choice but to go back to my own house and brood.

Chapter Twenty

As I walked in the back door, I reviewed my options. My nerves were jangling a warning that I'd already sent them into caffeine overload. I was too wired for a nap, in no mood to check out the package Pauline had dropped off and not desperate enough to seek refuge in a wine bottle so early in the day. Finally, I grabbed a book I'd been meaning to read and curled up in the hammock on the screened-in section of the front porch. But there was no escape from my thoughts.

From where I sat I could hear the slow, monotonous beat of the lake, but it didn't offer the usual feeling of serenity. Questions raced through my mind. What was the real story on Deke? How could Ramona, whose life was now in as much turmoil as her kitchen, find the strength to cope? And what had Mr. Roberts done that Jack found so upsetting? That phone call Friday afternoon seemed to spell even more trouble for the business. If it hadn't been for Rick Cronin's arrival at my house this morning, maybe Jack would have told me what was wrong.

As I thought back to the committee meeting the day before, I remembered something else--Tom Bailey's heavy-handed explanation about why he had been at the Taggerts' house that afternoon while Bob was working. Was there something going on between him and Melissa? If Tom hadn't tried so hard to explain his presence, I wouldn't have thought twice about it.

And another thing--what had turned my dinner with Don so sour? I wanted to blame Phil Johnson and his insistence on showing me the campground, but something else had altered the mood as well. Don had been sending out powerful signals, definite hints that he viewed the evening as more than a casual get together. My instincts hadn't atrophied so much I'd misread that message, had they? Then suddenly he was glad to be rid of me. Come to think of it,

Jim Thompson had been equally anxious to get rid of me this afternoon. Maybe it was time to change my shower soap.

"Is anyone home?" a voice called from the back door.

The question and the sharp knock which followed startled me. Relieved at the prospect of company, I hurried to the kitchen. Jeannie Spenser stood outside my screen. How did women like Jeannie do it, I wondered. Clothes still crisp and wrinkle-free, hair perfectly coifed, makeup recently freshened. But, as I opened the door, I saw exhaustion in her face. An expression of my grandmother's echoed in my mind. All the starch had gone out of her. I waited, expecting her to tell me Deke was dead.

She surprised me. "I'm so glad I've found you at home, Loren. I've just come from picking up some clothes for my mother-- I'm going to keep her at my house for a few days--and I couldn't wait another minute to stop by and apologize for the way I acted this morning."

I moved back from the door.

"Come in, Jeannie."

She stepped into the kitchen.

"I had no idea who you were. I assumed you were someone working for my mother or maybe a neighbor helping out. Thompson should have introduced us, saved me from handing out orders the way I did."

"Not a problem," I said.

"Well, of course it was. I let you go on cleaning that filthy kitchen, even instructed you about locking up the house. I was frightfully embarrassed when I found out you were the mayor up here. I've seen you around, I guess, but I didn't recognize you."

I could have explained that I hadn't been given time to change clothes, but I decided not to. After all, clothes didn't make the mayor--to paraphrase a bit--or anyone else, especially in Emerald Point, the casual dress capital of the Northeast. Jeannie should have learned that in her real estate business. I reached for another topic.

"Tell me how Deke is doing."

The floodgates of the dam burst open. Despite Jeannie's efforts to appear in control, she was close to falling apart. "Well, he's not dead, that's all I can say at this point, and I can't pretend I'd be heartbroken if he was. I'm sorry for my mother, of course. She won't leave the hospital, even though he's in intensive care and she only can see him for a few minutes every hour. But Deke has meant nothing but trouble to her."

I could see tears forming in her eyes. I wasn't up for coffee, so I did the hospitality thing by offering a glass of wine. A few minutes later, we sat on the porch, sipping glasses of Pinot Grigio as Jeannie unleashed a torrent of complaints about Deke Dolley and his role in her mother's life.

"I thought she'd be all set after my father's death if I helped her buy the motel. Then she brought that freeloader in on it."

I listened without comment. I'd viewed Deke as a big talker who exaggerated his own importance and Ramona as secure enough to let him do it. Like others in town, I'd figured her for the brains behind the business and Deke as an easy-going front man. Maybe I'd misjudged them both.

"I always thought they got along well," I said.

"Oh, getting along well with women is Deke's stock in trade. He's lived in the Lake George area for years; been involved with any number of older women who welcomed his attentions and could afford to pay for them."

"Deke, a gigolo? I never thought of him that way," I said.

"He courted Kitty Heinz for a while and Doris Reynolds, too. But they got wise to him. My mother was quite a comedown for him financially, but, when he took up with her, the motel was in good shape, a nice little money maker."

I tried not to look disbelieving. I couldn't reconcile Jeannie's words with the condition of the motel that morning.

"You're thinking I'm way off base, aren't you? But, ten years ago the motel looked a lot different. In those days Mother had great hopes."

Didn't we all ten years ago? But I didn't voice that thought. Jeannie Spenser struck me as a woman who'd achieved her own goals and had no patience with anyone who hadn't. I recalled the past due bills and the unpaid mortgage I'd seen on Ramona's dining room table.

"The motel business can be tough," I said.

Jeannie's words poured out. "Deke prattles on about seasonal downswings and local business conditions, but he's siphoned off large amounts of money and I don't know what he's used it for. I admit I've stayed away more than I should have because I couldn't stand listening to his grandiose remarks."

Jeannie continued her tirade and I didn't try to stop her. Maybe this was what she needed for a safety valve--this chance to express her anger and frustration. But as she talked, I was making connections I didn't want to make. Phil Johnson, Peter Finch, Jack's father, now Deke and Ramona, all apparently in financial trouble. Four local businesses with major problems--and at exactly the same time. Emerald Point might not attract as lively a tourist trade as Lake George Village, but we did have a steady influx of summer visitors. Tom Bailey, only a few miles down the road, claimed he'd never seen things so good. Maybe he should be sharing his secret with the others.

After Jeannie finished a second glass of wine and calmed down a little, I insisted on fixing her a ham and cheese sandwich and a cup of coffee. When she finally exhausted her complaints about Deke, I switched the subject.

"Jeannie, you mentioned local business conditions a few minutes ago. People credit you with the best sense of the area's economy. How do you assess the business climate in our community right now?"

Jeannie acknowledged the compliment with a knowing smile. After all, this was her area of expertise.

"You mean, right now, before the summer season gets much of a start? Not so different from other years. As you know, Loren, businesses all around the lake count heavily on good weather. They have to make their money in a few short weeks and that isn't always easy." She paused, waiting for me to ask something more specific.

I phrased my comment carefully. "I'm hearing rumors about Emerald Point motel and hotel owners with financial problems and I'm concerned. I'm not asking you to violate any confidences, but I'm wondering if those rumors have any basis in fact."

Jeannie drained her cup and stared at the wine bottle. I recognized a meaningful glance when I saw one. I got the bottle and refilled her glass.

"Well, there are always people, especially in that kind of business, who've saddled themselves with too much debt. As I say, a lot depends on how the summer goes," she said.

"Do you see signs of a slow-down, indications that our economy may be unraveling?"

"You're not thinking of selling your house, are you, Loren? My mother told me you once considered opening a Bed and Breakfast. Have you given up that idea?"

Not what I'd intended to talk about, but not a bad direction for our conversation to take.

"I'm still not sure what I'm going to do about that. If longtime business people are in trouble, what chance would a beginner have starting out in this economic climate?"

"Who have you heard is in trouble?" Jeannie frowned as if she couldn't imagine what I meant.

"Deke, of course, for one."

She made a dismissive gesture. "You can't equate Deke's problems with anyone else's. He was a very poor businessman. Mother let him handle way too much, far more than he was capable of."

"Then, there's Peter and Jane Finch, too. I hear disturbing rumors about them. They appeared to be doing great, even talked expansion. Now they seem to have problems." I was basing my comment on more than Peter's flare-up at the Inn. Rumors had been circulating all spring that the Finches were overextended.

"Exactly what have you heard?" Jeannie asked.

This wasn't the direction I wanted to go in. I had to get her to tell me, not the other way around.

"Financial troubles. You probably know more about that than I do," I said.

Jeannie nodded in a non-committal way. "Sometimes trying to expand too quickly can be a mistake."

"And yet that wouldn't explain Phil Johnson's problems at the Beach House, or..." I rumbled to a stop, reluctant to violate Jack's confidence by bringing up the Inn.

"I see where you're going with this, Loren. You don't want to mention the Emerald Point Inn, so I'll speak of it myself. In my work, I need to be tuned to what's happening on the lake and I've heard the talk. The old man's made some mistakes, but I'm sure they can be put right. Still, if you believe all these businesses are financially unstable, I can see why you'd be concerned."

I backed up fast.

"Unstable? I'm not willing to go that far," I said quickly, not sure I hadn't done that very thing. "I guess I'm still not used to the undercurrent of gossip making the rounds in a small town. On the other hand, Tom Bailey says he's never seen things so good. Makes me wonder who to believe."

"Oh, that's Tom's usual style. Put on a happy face and all that. But I wouldn't worry. As far as I know, Emerald Point is in good shape." She hesitated, flashed me a conspiratorial smile. "And with maybe some better things on the horizon I'm not at liberty to talk about just yet."

"Something better on the horizon? That sounds promising. So I'm concerned for nothing?"

"Loren, you've been very kind to my mother and I appreciate that. I can only assure you there's no need to worry. But really, I shouldn't even be saying that much." She set down her empty wine glass, signaling that our conversation was over.

I didn't move for a minute. I thought we'd just brushed against something significant, but I had no idea what it was. Were there really better things on the horizon for Emerald Point? I'd like to think so.

Jeannie stood up. "Thank you for your hospitality. I have to go."

I followed her out to her Volvo, relieved to see that she appeared none the worse for the wine. As I stood next to her car, I noticed a flat cardboard box filled with papers on the back seat. I recognized the documents on top as the ones I'd seen on Ramona's dining room table. Jeannie must have gotten permission from one of the sheriff's deputies to take them home with her. A good idea, I thought. Enough of Deke and Ramona's problems were going to become public. No need for their private papers to be left lying around their house for everyone to see.

Chapter Twenty-one

WHEN I WALKED back into the house after Jeannie left, I noticed the manila envelope still lying on the kitchen counter. For the first time I looked carefully at the outside. My name was scrawled on it in writing nothing like Pauline's neat penmanship. I pulled open the stapled end of the package and a small black notebook slid out. No name, no date, no indication of what the notebook contained. Todd Lewis had said he was sending me something of Tammy's. Maybe this was it. I reached a hand inside the envelope, hoping to find a note, but there was nothing there.

I handled the notebook gingerly, touching only the edges. I suspected this was Tammy Stevenson's notebook, the mysterious discovery Todd had made and insisted on sending me. He'd asked me to hold it for a few days before turning it in to the sheriff's department, but he hadn't told me not to examine it myself. I took a silver knife from the drawer and flipped the pages to the first one with writing. On it was an entry in a flowery script--a group of letters on one line and a series of numbers several spaces below.

I flipped to another page. Again, a combination of letters and numbers. Three other pages held similar entries. In the manner of adolescent girls, Tammy had kept a coded record of something. But what? Five entries all together, each on a separate right hand page. On four of the pages the numbers were followed by slanted lines, several spaces, then more numbers. One page had a smudge, possibly a question mark which had been erased.

I found a piece of paper and, still using the knife to turn the pages, I copied the letter/number combinations, hoping that seeing them together might help me decipher them. Nothing clicked. The writing was attractive, too fancy for the average adult, but the curlicues reminded me of the penmanship of teenage girls I'd known. I had no trouble believing that Tammy had made these notes.

I slid the notebook carefully back into the envelope and returned it to the counter. The next day was Sunday. I'd make a half-hearted effort to locate Jim, then take the package to him on Monday morning at his office. If I missed him, fine. I'd leave a note explaining how I'd come by it. I wouldn't be stretching the truth too much if I told him I hadn't opened the package right away. A simple plan--at least it seemed so at the time.

SUNDAY AFTERNOON THE town still buzzed with talk. By this time everyone had heard the coroner's findings. Tammy Stevenson had been beaten to death with a blunt instrument, possibly as much as a year ago, and her body hidden in a thick growth of vegetation. Her car had been driven off a nearby embankment at a speed high enough to clear rocks on the shore below and send it crashing into the water.

Then, as if that wasn't enough, only a few days after her body was found, Deke Dolley had attempted suicide. Speculating about a connection between the two events hit the top of the charts as everyone's favorite weekend activity.

"Of course, it's coincidence. It has to be," I said to Kate when I finally caught up with her at her house Sunday afternoon.

Kate shook her head, definitely not convinced. "I wonder. From what Josie tells me--and you know anything she chooses to reveal to me is only the tip of the iceberg--Tammy had links to more people than you'd believe possible."

"Are you saying she was linked to Deke? That can't be right," I said.

I hadn't repeated Jack's tale of attempted seduction and I didn't plan to tell even a close friend like Kate what he'd told me. But, was his experience an example of how Tammy forged those links? Not Deke, I thought. Surely not squat, unappealing Deke Dolley. Jim had indicated that Tammy had asked men for money to finance her way out of town. Deke didn't have spare cash to give away. I'd seen the past due bills, the signs that he and Ramona were in desperate straits. Unless... Maybe he had given Tammy money. Could gifts to a conniving young woman have contributed to Deke and Ramona's financial problems?

I could understand why Tammy might have wanted to seduce Jack. He was a good-looking guy in his early forties, attractive to women, maybe even a romantic figure to a young girl. But Deke Dolley?

"Deke and Tammy. No way," I said to Kate.

"Like you never heard of that combo before--older man, beautiful young girl? How about T*he Blue Angel, The Girl in the Red Velvet Swing*, Anna Nicole Smith? Get with the program, Loren. May/December relationships happen all the time."

I did a fast about face. "Of course. What am I thinking? That something like that couldn't happen in Emerald Point? I need a reality check."

CHAPTER TWENTY-TWO

THE FIRST THING Monday morning, I clipped a card with Jim's name on it to the manila envelope containing the little black notebook. Then, I delivered it to the receptionist at the Municipal Center and made a fast getaway. No sign of Jim or anyone else from the sheriff's department. My duty was done.

Not for long. An hour later Melissa Taggert telephoned my office to extend a special invitation to the memorial service she was planning for Tammy. Her family and friends had talked her out of an elaborate funeral, she explained. She'd settled, instead, on a small, private memorial at a Lake George funeral home the following day. I hemmed a little, but I knew there was no way to avoid going.

Pauline seconded my decision. "She really wants you there," she said that afternoon when I told her about Melissa's call, "and you'd never forgive yourself if you didn't go. I can come in early."

Tuesday morning I stood just inside the front door of the McTavish Funeral Home in Lake George Village and waited for my eyes to adjust to the gloom inside. The large room was decorated in somber hues, the windows covered in thick, burgundy velvet drapes. I took a seat midway down the rows of chairs which had been set up for the service. Several small groups of mourners had already gathered--a scattering of teenage girls, Allison and another woman, a few couples I assumed were friends or relatives.

A few minutes before eleven Melissa led her family in. She wore a simple black sheath, her auburn hair caught back in a silver clip. Bob, neatly dressed in a dark suit, white shirt and maroon tie, followed a half step behind her. Chrissie, Tammy's thirteen-year-old half sister, plodded along after them in an outfit she'd apparently chosen for its shock value--a black mini skirt and halter top which left quantities of bare, jiggley flesh exposed. I wondered how much Chrissie really knew about Tammy's life and death and if she was in danger of going that same route. Even Rob, the sloppy young guy I'd seen passing out hors d'oeuvres at the Chamber meeting, had dressed up for the occasion in a navy blazer and khaki slacks. He led a little blonde girl in a pretty summer dress down the aisle--the youngest Taggert, I assumed--and settled her in the row behind Melissa and Bob.

One of the Lake George music teachers, whose name I couldn't come up with, played several hymns on the funeral home's small organ. Rustling sounds from the back of the room indicated that more people were arriving. As the last notes of *Amazing Grace* died away, the Reverend John Sanford stood to offer the eulogy.

"Today, we are mourning the untimely death of a lovely young woman, sharing this loss with her grieving family," he began. He'd prepared his message with care. He concentrated on the family's sorrow, the brevity of Tammy's life, the hope she was at peace.

When he completed his remarks, he motioned to a girl who'd taken a seat in the front row.

"This is Denise Templeton, a friend of Tammy's," Reverend Sanford said by way of introduction. "She asked if she could sing a hymn which was a favorite of Tammy's when they sang in the grade school choir together."

Denise, painfully ill at ease, shuffled to the front of the room and sang *Abide With Me* in a wavery contralto. The sounds of sniffling behind me revealed I wasn't the only one moved by her valiant effort. *Fast falls the eventide.* The eventide had claimed the little choir girl much too quickly. After a moment of silence, which gave us time to dry our eyes, Reverend Sanford concluded the service.

As I made my way out of the funeral home squinting into the bright sunlight, Melissa hurried up to me.

"Thanks for being here. Please come to our home for the luncheon. Everything will be ready when we get there."

Once again, I couldn't refuse.

At the Taggerts' house the dining room table had been pushed back almost to the wall. Several women stood behind it, ready to serve the salads, casseroles, meats and breads displayed in front of them.

"Hi, Mayor. Nice of you to come," Allison called over her shoulder as she dashed in and took her place with the other servers. I liked her game plan--we'd pretend our disagreement at Kate's dinner party had never taken place. Maybe I should suggest this approach to warring Common Council members.

I helped myself to a cup of coffee and a plate of food and sat down on a folding chair under the archway in the dining room. From this vantage point I could observe almost everything happening in the downstairs. As the Taggerts' friends and neighbors crowded in, most of the men headed directly for the kitchen. I heard the pop of beer cans being opened and the clink of glasses and bottles.

The relatives gathered in the living room. I picked out the women I thought were Bob's sisters. The talk in that room was subdued, in marked contrast to the noisy chatter emanating from the kitchen.

Kate slipped into the chair next to me. "Did you try my Harvest potatoes? I used a new recipe for them and I like the way they came out."

"You brought something?" I said.

"I sent it down earlier. People sort of expect it of me now. And I did want to do something. There but for the grace of God, you know."

"Not from what I've been hearing. You may feel you have your hands full with Josie, but she's not in Tammy's league."

"I hope not. I've been hearing some pretty scary stuff myself."

The sounds drifting in from the kitchen grew more raucous.

"Sports," I whispered to Kate, "the safe, universal male topic, suitable for any occasion, guaranteed to keep everyone from delving too deep or revealing emotion."

"Oops, a little edgy this morning, are we?" Kate asked with a sympathetic smile.

"I'm still not sure I understand this kind of gathering," I went on. "Let's see. The women prepare and serve food and clean up afterward. The men guzzle beer. The guests aren't expected to act too gloomy, but they aren't supposed to laugh uproariously or have too good a time either. I don't think the gang in the kitchen quite gets that last part."

"Didn't you attend events like this in New York?"

"I guess I must have, but they were usually held in restaurants and there was a certain formality. But no matter, I've got to get going." I slid my plate and cup onto a tray of dirty dishes on a small table nearby. I was planning my exit strategy when Melissa headed me off.

"Please wait just a minute. Bob wants to talk to you," she said.

"No, I really have to go," I insisted. I didn't want an apology or, worst yet, a continuation of our exchange the night he'd surprised me outside my door. I wanted him to do exactly what Allison had done--move on.

Melissa ignored my comment and hurried into the kitchen. Through the open door, I saw Bob and Tom Bailey standing together, their attention focused on someone out of my line of vision. I felt as if I'd hit the mute button on a television as I watched their expressions change, their anger escalate. Tom's cheeks reddened as the blood flooded into his face. The others in the kitchen didn't notice what was happening but droned on about sports and summer business problems.

Tom Bailey took a step forward, his face twisted in rage. He clenched his fists, ready to take a swing at the person provoking him.

Kate gripped my arm as she stared into the part of the kitchen I couldn't see. "Loren, there's going to be a fight and Jack's right in the thick of it."

"Jack is out there?" I leaned toward her, craning my neck to see. Jack, apparently as angry as Tom, stood glowering at him from across the room.

Tom Bailey's shout sliced through the general din. "Don't threaten me, you arrogant bastard!"

The noise level in the room dropped as the other men realized a fight was brewing. To my surprise, Bob Taggert assumed the role of peacemaker. He reached for Tom's arm, stepped between him and Jack. Jack wheeled around suddenly and disappeared. I heard the slam of a door, then a few seconds of silence followed by a rising crescendo of voices asking the inevitable questions.

"Kate, make my apologies to Melissa. Tell her I had to leave," I said as I started for the front door.

No one noticed my departure. Attention was focused on the kitchen where the men were speculating about what had provoked the argument.

As I rushed out of the house, I saw Jack hurrying down the street toward his car. I caught up with him as he opened the door.

"Jack, what was that all about?"

"I can't talk now. If I don't get away from here, I'll go back in there and kill Tom Bailey." He slid into his car and yanked the door shut. Without so much as a glance in my direction, he started the engine and took off.

My own temper flared, but I tried to suspend judgment. Jack had mentioned the Inn's financial problems, but without giving details. Jeannie Spenser had spoken of mistakes Mr. Roberts had made. Was Tom Bailey somehow connected to those mistakes?

Something was wrong, very wrong.

CHAPTER TWENTY-THREE

BY THE TIME I pulled away from the Taggerts' house a few minutes later, I'd formulated my own plan of action. I gave Pauline a quick call on my cell phone. "I'm not coming back this afternoon. If anyone's looking for me, say I've gone to Glens Falls to see Ramona at the hospital."

As I drove along the Northway, I sifted through the events of the last few days. I remembered the advice Dianne Feinstein had once given to other women mayors "You have to learn the rules of the game, and then play it better than anyone else," she'd told them.

Her advice made sense. Emerald Point might be a long way from San Francisco, but I'd realized soon after my election exactly how right she was.

What Dianne hadn't spelled out for me was that before I could learn the rules of the game, I'd better figure out what they were. In this strange game we seemed to be playing, the rules were nebulous. Everybody knew something, but nobody knew everything--like a card game where you saw your own cards and were expected to make an educated guess about what the other players were holding.

Jack acknowledged that his father had messed up somehow, but he wasn't about to reveal how or why--at least not to me. I considered him a friend and I thought he saw me the same way. But Jack, as secretive these days as a CIA operative, was playing his cards close to his vest.

Jim Thompson, a classic example of the strong, poker-faced lawman, obviously knew more about Tammy Stevenson's murder and Deke Dolley's suicide attempt than he was willing to divulge. He'd be a tough nut to crack but, if I kept my wits about me, maybe, just maybe, I'd find some way to open him up.

Then, there was Deke Dolley. Apparently Deke, overwhelmed by his business problems, had taken the only way out he could think of--suicide. Except poor Deke, who wasn't very good at anything, hadn't been very good at that either.

And what role did Tom Bailey play in all this? What was his relationship to Melissa Taggert and what had he said or done to cause Jack to explode like that in the Taggerts' kitchen?

Since I didn't have the foggiest idea what was happening, I had two choices. I could stumble along in the dark or jump in with both feet and try to figure out what was going on. The second course of action might ruffle a few feathers, but I'd done that before and survived. Why should this time be any different?

When I reached the hospital, I went directly to the Intensive Care Unit and found Ramona sitting on a straight chair just inside the entrance.

"Ramona, how is he?" I asked.

She looked at me with the same blank expression I'd seen on her face Saturday morning.

"No change, Loren. He's so pale and quiet. It's almost like he's dead already."

"What do the doctors say?"

"Nothing. Nothing at all."

I patted her hand. "Let me take you down to the cafeteria for some lunch."

"Thanks, but I don't want to leave here. I can only see him for five minutes every hour and it's time for me to go in again." She pushed herself up from the chair.

The ICU was a large room with a center island holding an impressive array of monitors and machines whose beeps and read-outs kept the nurses on duty informed of their patients' conditions. Ramona walked around the counter and entered one of the small, glass-walled cubicles located along the opposite wall. I could see her through the window as she bent to kiss Deke's forehead.

As I stood watching her, one of the nurses came over to me.

"Ms. Graham? I'm Bobbie Smith. I live at Emerald Point."

"Bobbie, I'm glad to see you here. Tell me how Deke is doing. Ramona doesn't seem to know much."

Bobbie considered the best way to answer my question. Unlike many of the new wave of nurses, she wore a crisp, white uniform and a starched manner--very much the professional.

"Mr. Dolley's still unconscious. We're doing all we can for him, of course, but I'm concerned about Mrs. Dolley. She sits here all day, just sits and watches his cubicle. She won't even go out into the waiting room, gets upset when her daughter comes for her. I'm afraid she's going to make herself sick."

"Is there a chance of Deke's regaining consciousness? Is that why she wants to be here?" I asked.

She shook her head. "That's hard to say. Maybe you could talk to her, get her to spare herself a little. If he does regain consciousness, he'll need her with him then more than he does now."

"Ramona," I said when she returned. "You can't go in again for almost an hour. Let's go downstairs for something to eat."

Ramona shook her head.

I tried again a few minutes later, but nothing I said would persuade her to leave her post. I accepted defeat and went downstairs to the cafeteria to get her a sandwich and a cup of coffee.

When I came back, Jeannie Spenser stood next to her mother, waiting for me. "How very kind of you, Loren. Mother can take this with her and eat in the car. I have to bring her home now."

Ramona let out a strangled cry. "Oh no. It's too early, Jeannie. Can't you find somebody to pick me up later? If you'd let me get my own car..."

Jeannie ignored her mother's protests and addressed her remarks to me. "My husband and I are attending a real estate banquet tonight. I told Mother about it earlier. I must get her home and make sure she's had something to eat before I leave for the evening."

"Jeannie, I don't want to stay at your house all alone. Let me stay here. Please."

Butt out, I told myself, but I couldn't stand hearing Ramona beg. "Can I help in some way? Maybe I could come down and get her later."

Jeannie glowered at me as if I'd just made a ridiculously low offer on a house. "No. Not at all. We go through this every day. The desk will call her if there's any change."

Jeannie seized her mother's elbow and pushed her toward the elevator. Ramona shuffled along, looking back over her shoulder as if pleading with me to do something. A feeling of powerlessness washed over me. I felt as if I were abandoning an abused child.

After the elevator doors had closed behind Jeannie and Ramona, I approached the desk where Bobbie Smith was filling in a chart.

"Is there anything I could be doing for Ramona?" I asked her.

She shook her head. "Mrs. Dolley would stay here all day and all night if her daughter would let her. I think she's afraid her husband is going to die and she won't be with him."

"Is he going to die? Is his condition that serious?" I asked her.

Bobbie retreated quickly. "Oh, I didn't mean to imply that he was, just that Mrs. Dolley acts so frightened all the time, I assume that's what she's thinking."

Some card player I was. As I fled the Intensive Care Unit, relieved to escape its somber atmosphere with its cacophony of bells and whistles, I admitted defeat. I hadn't learned one thing I didn't know when I arrived. Fortunately, I had another idea.

Chapter Twenty-four

WITH THE AFTERNOON free, I decided to make another stop--this time at Todd Lewis's parents' house.

I'd jotted down Todd's address and I had no trouble finding the development where the house was located, a section of one-story homes on the northern edge of Lake George Village. A slim woman in khaki shorts and a white tee, a woman who bore such a striking resemblance to Todd she had to be his mother, was weeding a bed of impatiens in front of a small, yellow bungalow.

She stood up and brushed the dirt from her long, tanned legs. I told her who I was.

"Oh yes. I appreciated your call about Todd. He did, too. He's a funny kid. He pretended it was no big deal, but I could tell how much it pleased him."

I played dumb--not much of a stretch for me at this point.

"Is he home now?"

"No. Do you want him for some reason?"

"I would like to talk to him. When will he be home?"

Mrs. Lewis pushed back a lock of damp hair, streaking dirt across her face. She leaned over and fussed with an assortment of gardening tools, rearranging them carefully in a small, wheeled cart. When she finally spoke, she didn't answer my question. Instead, she asked, "Would you like to come in for a cold drink?"

She'd made a decision: she was going to tell me something. I thanked her and followed her into the house.

Bella Lewis and I sat at the table in her neat little kitchen and sipped from tall glasses of iced tea. The heat was oppressive after the air conditioning in the car and at the hospital. The sky had darkened, signaling that a storm was building. Thunder showers often bombarded the lake at this time of year, unleashing powerful winds and wild light shows that set the skies on fire.

I waited for Bella Lewis to speak about Todd. We toyed with other subjects until we finally arrived at Tammy Stevenson's death.

"I almost went to the service today, but then I didn't think it would be a very good idea," Bella said.

"Why? Was it because Todd was there when her body was found? You don't think people suspect him, do you?" I couldn't hold back my questions any longer. Maybe I was moving too fast, but I had to find out what she'd decided to tell me.

She didn't let me rush her. "Not exactly. Todd's afraid he's in a lot of trouble. His father and I have no idea how to advise him." She hesitated again, waiting for me to ask the question.

I went for it. "Why trouble?"

Instead of answering, Bella Lewis excused herself and left the room. I heard the sound of a drawer being pulled open and slid shut. She returned dangling a brown leather shoulder bag by its strap.

"Todd found this pocketbook right near where you found the body. He looked into it. Then afterward, he was afraid to turn it in for fear his fingerprints would be on it. He hid it under a big rock. Later he went and got it and brought it home."

It was the missing *Coach* bag Melissa had asked about. I could see the brand name, clearly visible.

"How did he manage that? I heard they put a guard up there until after they finished searching."

Bella bit down hard on her lip. "I don't know. That's what he told me."

And of course, it was possible he'd done just that, guard or no guard. Josie could have pulled off something like this. Probably any other self-respecting teenager could have done it, too.

So this was the *Coach* bag Melissa Taggert had been looking for. The notebook wasn't the only thing Todd had found that day. I remembered how he'd hugged his midsection. I'd thought he was hurting from his fall; maybe he'd been clutching the bag under his shirt.

"Bella, this is serious. He may have destroyed clues that could tell them who killed Tammy. Why would he do such a thing? Unless..." Unless Todd had killed her himself. Maybe Jim had been onto something when he questioned me about Todd's behavior that morning.

My comment brought her close to tears. The streaks of dirt on her face made her appear young and vulnerable as if she were the frightened teenager who'd done something stupid.

"I don't know what he was thinking. His father and I are wrecks about this. Todd may have ruined his whole life, taking off the way he did. You can't run from your problems. We've always insisted that he face up to things and now..."

"Why are you telling me this? What do you expect me to do with this information?" I spoke more sharply than I meant to, but she'd put me in an awful spot. I'd already held off on turning over the notebook to Jim. I couldn't mess around with something else.

"You work closely with Jim Thompson sometimes. Could you take the pocketbook to him and try to make him understand why Todd kept it? Tell him Todd was afraid they'd think he killed Tammy."

As if Jim hadn't considered the possibility already. I tried to tap into the investigator's way of thinking. I didn't have a choice here, I was sure he'd tell me. If I refused to take the bag and Bella and her husband destroyed it, any chance of finding fingerprints or other clues would be gone.

"Come with me to the Municipal Center and we'll do it right now," I said.

"No. No. I can't. Really I can't do it and neither can my husband. If you won't help us, we'll get a lawyer and see what he tells us to do."

That could hold things up indefinitely. I felt sure Jim would prefer the first course of action.

"I'll take it," I told her.

Bella Lewis pulled a plastic grocery bag from the top shelf of her broom closet and slid the pocketbook into it.

"Here's a letter Todd started to write you. He was going to send the pocketbook to you and then he changed his mind."

I flicked the folded paper open and read the scribbled message aloud.

Mayor Graham, I heard today Tammy was murdered. I found this pocketbook on the hill near where the car went in. I sent you the little notebook and hid the rest. I'm afraid they'll find my fingerprints and think I killed her. Give me a couple days head start before you show this to anybody. P.S. I took the money out of her wallet, too.

"How much money?" I snapped the question at Bella Lewis. "You've got to tell me. It could make a difference, really it could."

Bella shook her head. "He didn't tell us. That's the truth, I swear it. He didn't tell us."

Had robbery been a motive? Could Todd have killed Tammy for money? I picked up the bag.

Bella Lewis followed me to the front door, visibly shaken.

"Bella," I said in what I hoped was a calmer tone of voice, "I don't like Todd's role in this either, but you've done the right thing. I'll be in touch."

As soon as I'd driven away from the house, I had second thoughts, big ones. I didn't regret taking the pocketbook--I figured I'd had to do that--but I should have tried harder to get Todd's mother to go to the sheriff's department with me. Not only would Jim be furious over the notebook, he'd really blow his top when I arrived with this new piece of evidence. Maybe he'd already been trying to contact me. I pulled off the road and called both my office and the house, pushing the buttons on my cell phone which connected me with my answering machines. Sure enough. I heard Jim's voice, cold as death, crackle from both machines.

"Mayor Graham, call me the minute you get this message."

At least I'd have a better excuse when I turned over the pocketbook. I couldn't leave it behind, I'd tell him. I couldn't take a chance that Bella Lewis might reconsider and destroy it.

I glanced at my watch. A little after six. Jim was probably somewhere between work and home. I had a few minutes grace.

Although sunset was more than two hours away, the light had drained out of the sky fading it to an ominous gray. Fierce looking clouds scudded low over the lake. The soft June air took on a cold, clammy feel as if it blew out of the basement of the world. Flashes of lightning zigzagged across the sky, one after the other. I jumped at an especially loud clap of thunder.

Ramona. She hated thunderstorms and she hadn't wanted to stay alone at Jeannie's anyway. I pictured her cowering in a chair, terrified, even more distraught than she'd been at the hospital. I was only a short distance from where Jeannie lived. I took the turn leading to Lake Shore Drive.

Jeannie Spenser and her husband, a silent and--according to local gossip--not very effective partner in her real estate agency, had started restoring their home on the lake a few years ago, shortly after I moved to Emerald Point. The remodeling had provided hours of speculation for area residents, not just in Lake George Village but in nearby towns as well. The nineteenth century home didn't make the cut as one of what folks here called the *great and gracious* lakeside mansions, but Jeannie, known for her sharp eye, had recognized its potential. She'd hired the best architect she could find and embarked on a program to remodel, re-landscape and--unkind tongues added-- re-mortgage the house, all without destroying its innate charm.

Even the winding driveway I followed in from the highway was a masterpiece of planning. My own new parking area took a considerable drop in my estimation as I drove under a portico and got out of my car.

By this time the storm was roaring down the lake like a locomotive at full throttle. The wind threatened to knock me off the low step by the side door. The house loomed above me, dark and foreboding in the half-light. I rang the bell and rapped my knuckles on the wooden door. No response from inside the house, but I felt as if someone was lurking in the bushes behind me, watching me. I banged again, even harder this time. I saw one of the curtains lifted aside by an unseen hand. "Ramona, is that you? It's Loren. Let me in."

The curtain settled back into place and I heard the sound of a key turning in a lock.

"Jeannie told me not to let anyone in, but she didn't mean you," Ramona said as she cracked the door just wide enough for me to slip through.

"I wanted to make sure you were all right," I said.

Ramona made sure the door had locked, then threw her arms around me. Her cheeks were streaked with dried tears, her eyes were red rimmed and haunted.

"Oh, Loren, I'm so glad you're here. Thank you for coming. Thank you."

"Has Jeannie left for her dinner?" I asked.

"Yes. She insisted on fixing me something before she left. I don't know why she bothers. I can't eat anyway."

I hadn't noticed at the hospital how much weight Ramona had lost. When had this happened? Ramona had been short and plump, bustling about at community events like an energetic pouter pigeon. Now her face looked gaunt and her clothes hung loosely on her small frame.

She led me into a small den. I could see a news program on television, but she had clicked the mute button and we sat in silence listening to the storm hit. Rain swept off the lake, pelting the windows. The house shuddered from the force of the wind. Lightning flashed and monstrous claps of thunder bombarded us. I could sense Ramona's trembling. I moved over next to her on the couch and took her hand.

"Loren, you don't know. I'm so scared. Everything is so awful." Her words came out in quick bursts of sound. Her eyes had a wild, unfocused look that scared me.

"Is Jeannie's dinner at the Lake George Club? I'm going to call her," I said.

"No. No. She'll be mad."

I put my arm around Ramona, holding her close. Suddenly, all the windows lit up with a brilliant flash of lightning. The simultaneous roar of thunder almost knocked us off the couch. The lamp in the den went out. The picture on the television screen shrunk to a small dot and vanished.

"The power's off. It'll come right back on," I said with more assurance than I felt.

Ramona, shaking even more, began the same low keening sound she'd made on the porch the morning Deke had been shot. I hugged her to me, trying to calm her, but she rocked slowly back and forth, staring straight ahead into the darkness.

As soon as the lights came on, I went to the phone and put in a call to Jeannie. I didn't sugarcoat the situation. "Your mother's in bad shape. I think you should come home. She shouldn't be here alone."

To my surprise, Jeannie agreed at once. "I'll come right away. Could you stay twenty minutes more until I get there?" she said.

The television sputtered back to life. I clicked through the channels looking for something Ramona might watch, but she was sunk deep in her own thoughts. A sitcom I knew she liked, my efforts at conversation, nothing seemed to rouse her.

The minute I heard a key in the lock, I jumped to my feet, ready to defend my decision to call Jeannie home. But there was no need.

She rushed in, flinging her lightweight raincoat over a chair.

"Thank goodness, you stopped by, Loren. I didn't feel right about leaving Mother alone, but I was scheduled to speak at the dinner."

"The storm was too much for her," I said. "I thought she seemed very upset today at the hospital and I know she hates thunder and lightning. So I decided to check on her."

Jeannie went over to where Ramona sat huddled on the couch.

"Mother, what is it? What's wrong? Clint stayed at the dinner. He'll take care of making our announcement. Don't worry about it. It'll be all right."

Ramona stared straight ahead. Couldn't Jeannie see that she wasn't worried about the dinner or the announcement or how it was handled? Something else was bothering her, something that had her almost crazed with fear.

Chapter Twenty-five

By the time I left Jeannie Spenser's house, the storm had rolled down the lake, disappearing as quickly as it had struck. The somber gray which had enveloped everything such a short time before yielded to a soft luminescence, topped off by patches of blue sky and the first rose flush of sunset. The trees dripped moisture; the macadam steamed as the warm air dried up the puddles on the road. As soon as I was out of sight of the house, I stopped and called Jim Thompson.

I reached his answering machine at home and again at the Municipal Center. I left the same message each time.

"Jim, you're obviously tied up so I won't call again tonight. I'll be in your office first thing tomorrow morning." I felt as if I'd received a death house reprieve from the governor. I'd worry about Jim tomorrow.

I didn't agonize over the pros and cons of what I decided to do next. I drove to the Emerald Point Inn and walked quickly into the bar before I could change my mind. Jack's father was sitting on a barstool talking to Peter Finch and another man who looked vaguely familiar. The stranger--I assumed he must be a summer guest--sported the regulation khaki slacks and short-sleeved white sport shirt favored by visitors to the hotel. But, instead of the sneaks or moccasins which usually accompanied such an outfit, he wore heavy cordovan wing tips.

Mr. Roberts greeted me with a cheery smile. I wouldn't have pegged him as a man with serious financial problems.

"John, haven't seen much of you lately. How are you?" I asked him.

John swung his stool around and faced me.

"Good for an old geezer," he said, falling back on a common Emerald Point response I'd promised myself never to use.

"I wondered if Jack was around."

"Up in his apartment, I think. We're trading places tonight. I get to be in charge of the downstairs for a change and he stays put in his room."

An odd remark. Was I suppose to read something into it? "Maybe I'll run up, then."

"Good luck. You'll need it."

Sometimes Jack's father came across as the nicest guy in the world. At other times--well, I figured him for a drinker. He hid it well, but occasionally, like tonight, I had trouble knowing what he was implying.

On the way upstairs, I planned my conversation with Jack. We'd have a glass of wine. I'd let him do the talking, give him the chance to tell me why he was so upset. Apparently, his father had made some poor business decisions. Jack had started to tell me about them Saturday morning in my kitchen, but we'd been interrupted. He'd asked if I knew anyone at the bank. Maybe there'd be a way I could help. At least, I was willing to try. We'd put our disagreement about the meeting behind us and figure out what to do. I knocked on the door of the suite Jack had converted into his personal living quarters.

He opened the door in his shirt sleeves, glaring at me over the tops of his glasses. "Loren, what are you doing here?"

Not the warmest of welcomes, but I let it roll over me. "I wanted to see how you were. You seemed so upset earlier. I was concerned."

"It's nothing I want to discuss with you. I thought I made that clear." He spoke in the cold, clipped tones I'd heard him use on troublemakers in the bar. He continued to block the doorway.

"Okay, so we won't discuss it. May I come in anyway?"

"I'm really in the middle of something." He gestured behind him at the paper-strewn coffee table in front of the couch. A highball glass and a fifth of Canadian Club sat on the table next to the papers. I smelled liquor on his breath.

"Jack, what's wrong?"

"Believe me, you don't want to know."

My patience evaporated. So much for good intentions. "For God's sake, Jack. Cut the melodrama and tell me what's wrong."

"Loren, trust me on this. You don't want to know. Now go along." He reached out his hand and rested it on the edge of the door. As I watched in disbelief, he moved the door forward, pushing it slowly toward me, shutting me out of his room as emphatically as he was shutting me out of his life.

"Gottcha," I said. "I may not catch on fast, but sooner or later I get the message."

I swung around so quickly I almost tripped on the thick hall carpet. Before I'd taken my first step, I heard the door click shut behind me. When I got things wrong, I got them really wrong.

ONE GREAT ADVANTAGE of living in Emerald Point was that when you didn't want to go home, you didn't have to agonize over where to go instead. On a week night in early June, before the summer season hit in earnest, Mario's Pizzeria was the only game in town.

The cheerful little bar might be best known for its pizza, but it served a myriad of other community needs as well. *A clean, well-lighted place*, Hemingway would have called it. Signs in the window promised a full bar, tables for ladies, live music on weekends and a dozen different kinds of toppings. After my really bad day, Mario's pizza came as close to therapy as I could hope for.

The bartender, slouching behind the bar, gave me a wave as I walked in. The half dozen men perched on the stools were dedicating themselves to a sporting event of some kind on television. Three couples ate pizza at the tables in front. Not exactly a big night, even for Emerald Point.

As I debated whether or not to stay, Don Morrison swung around on one of the stools, bounced to his feet and came toward me smiling. I found myself grinning back. Did I appear overjoyed to see him? I'm sure he didn't miss my reaction.

"Are you here alone?" we both asked at almost the same moment. Definitely an evening on the upswing.

Don suggested a booth. I agreed quickly, embarrassingly so. He picked up his beer, signaled to a waitress and we walked to the back of the restaurant. In the next few minutes, I ordered the glass of wine I'd been hoping for earlier; Don decided on another beer; and we negotiated a compromise on pizza splitting. Final decision--half mushroom for me, half sausage for Don.

"What are you doing so far from home?" I asked him.

"Do you realize there's no place in Lake George Village where you can go for a drink and a late supper without running into a crowd? I checked out a couple of my favorite hangouts, found a mob scene and kept moving north."

"Mob scenes already, and not even the weekend. Stick a knife in my heart and be done with it. How do they do it?"

"They've been at it for years, remember? Lake George Village is an established destination. Folks up here at Emerald Point are finally acknowledging they need to attract more tourists, but they can't expect to do it overnight. It's going to take time."

We talked easily about tourism or the lack of it, why people chose certain vacation spots and overlooked others. Eventually we worked our way around to the meeting on the community center.

"The center's a good idea," Don said. "Too bad everything fizzed out that day, especially when I thought we were finally starting to get somewhere. Roberts was preoccupied, but I hear he's got other things on his mind right now."

"Like what?" I wasn't above probing for information on Jack's mysterious problems.

He waited until the waitress had set our drinks on the table and turned away. "The old man for one. He's not too sharp these days, they say. He's lost some tour groups, made some bad moves."

"Tour groups?" Was that what Jack had been so concerned about? There had to be something else wrong, didn't there?

"Poor business practices, too," Don continued. "I've heard the father had his sales manager giving great rates to attract new groups, then jacking up prices on their longtime accounts. As you can imagine, that didn't go over with the regulars."

"But how serious a matter is this? All businesses have their ups and downs around here."

"People make it sound serious. Maybe your friend has his reasons for being concerned, but he could use some lessons in running a meeting."

"He's not exactly a friend of mine right now." I'd blurted out the words before I could stop myself.

"Should I ask why?" Don asked with a smile.

"No. It's been a hectic day and there's something else I'd rather talk to you about. What do you hear about Deke Dolley?"

Don thought for a minute before he answered my question.

"No change in his condition, the last I heard. Mixed reports on what happened. He attempted suicide, I guess, but under somewhat suspicious circumstances. You probably know more than I do."

"Jim Thompson sent for me Saturday morning, mostly to give Ramona support. It looked like Deke had tried to kill himself, but you're right--there was some confusion about it."

As I said the words, I thought back to the conversation at the Dolley house that morning. What had Ramona been saying--that she'd heard voices, thought that someone had been out in the cabin with Deke? Jim had pushed her a little and she'd recanted. Then, Jeannie had provided a reason for her mother's story. She'd asked about the insurance, asked if Ramona was afraid the insurance wouldn't pay if Deke committed suicide.

"Do you know what they concluded?" Don said.

I shook my head. The waitress set our pizza and plates on the table and we each helped ourselves to a slice. My mind was racing. Ramona had seemed so frightened, not letting Deke out of her sight at the hospital, shaking with fear as she opened the door for me at Jeannie's house. What if she really had heard someone in the cabin that morning, someone who hadn't succeeded in killing Deke then and who might come back to finish the job? Maybe she feared they were both in danger. That scenario would explain her distraught state, her terrified watch at the hospital. But why would Jim fail to explore that possibility?

I pulled myself back to the present.

"I'm going to see Jim in the morning on another matter. I'll have some questions for him, you can bet on that," I said.

"And will he answer them?"

"You know, I've learned something about Jim. He doesn't always volunteer information, but he doesn't lie to me either. When I ask him a direct question, he answers it--or at least he answers with as much information as he wants to reveal at the time."

That was true. But, would Jim tell me what he really knew about Deke's shooting? Maybe the impression I'd gotten was the exact opposite of the truth. I'd thought Ramona had claimed to hear someone in the cabin in an effort to cover up Deke's suicide attempt. But, wasn't it possible she'd gone along with the suicide story to hide the fact that someone really had tried to kill him? Except, of course, that made no sense at all.

I shoved Ramona and Deke as far back in my mind as I could and switched us to another subject.

"Don, you seem to be in the loop on the late-breaking news around here. Anything more on Tammy Stevenson's murder?"

"Well, if you'll allow me to speak ill of the dead--people are saying very harsh things about her. A tough little tart. Old beyond her years. Linked with quite a few men as I understand it. Some choice gossip making the rounds."

I bristled, although I'd heard the same things.

"People seem to forget she was only seventeen years old. I hate the things I've heard," I said.

"You're sympathetic, but it may be sympathy wasted. That girl was trouble," he responded.

"So they tell me." Even Don was repeating the party line on Tammy. Or, was it only the male party line? I'd have to get Kate's reaction.

Don suggested another wine, but I did a quick recap of how my head felt after my last evening with him and ordered a cup of coffee instead.

"Want the rest of your pizza?" he asked.

"No, you take it with yours," I said as the waitress removed the leftover pizza from the table and prepared to wrap it.

"I love pizza for breakfast," Don said, "although I'll have to pick those mushrooms off. I hate those little buggers."

"You pick them off? Isn't that extreme?"

"Of course, if we were having breakfast together, we could split our leftovers and have no problem." His captivating smile made me wonder why I felt obliged to reject that idea.

"Actually, leftover pizza sounds better than what I'll be doing first thing in the morning. I'm scheduled for a meeting with Jim Thompson and he's ready to slap me in irons. I'm not looking forward to it."

"I've been turned down for some mighty demoralizing reasons, but this one's a real ego-buster. A dressing down by the sheriff's investigator preferred over pizza in bed with me. I can't tell you how offended I am."

He smiled that smile again, full wattage, powerful enough to start me considering ways I could put off the meeting. Would a sharp guy like Jim accept car trouble, a malfunctioning alarm clock, an unexpected phone call? Probably not. There was no way out, even if I'd been sure I wanted to find one.

CHAPTER TWENTY-SIX

AT SIX-THIRTY TUESDAY morning a relentless caterwauling drilled into my brain until I unstuck my eyelids and forced them open. The phone. The sun poured in through the little windows over the porch. Ordinarily, that much bright morning light would have brought me back to consciousness all by itself, but a long night of tossing and turning had left me dead to the usual stimuli. I groped along the nightstand. Jack, calling to apologize. I picked up the receiver.

"Mayor, I just want to make sure you're coming in for our meeting." Jim Thompson's voice sounded as cold as it had on my answering machines.

"Jim, for God's sake, I said I'd be there and I will. Bug off." As a rule, I tried not to be rude to anyone in law enforcement, especially Jim, but a call at that hour was enough to change my policy.

After an extra long shower and my requisite two cups of coffee--I was sure Jim would offer one more cup and that would put me in perfect shape--I scanned a group of better-than-average summer outfits in my closet. I decided on a pale green, two-piece dress, which looked like linen but wouldn't wrinkle even if Jim decided to grill me under the lights. I paid special attention to my hair, already curling from the humidity, and dabbed on an extra touch of makeup. Then-- and hey, why not--a quick spritz of a delicate floral scent. Use what you've got, they always say. Jim did it. He'd be neatly turned out in a freshly pressed blazer, the button under his dark tie fastened, black shoes gleaming obsidian-like from under his desk.

I drove by my office, hung up my *Back in 30* sign and crossed my fingers that the sign told the truth. At five minutes of eight, I took the package containing the *Coach* bag out of my trunk and walked into the sheriff's office at the County Municipal Center.

"Early enough for you, Jim?" I said as I tapped on his door and pushed it open. I didn't wait for an invitation to enter his office. He'd already extended one on the phone, hadn't he?

My entrance caught him off balance, I was happy to see.

"Coffee?" he asked.

"Love it," I said.

While he was still at the coffee maker, I launched into my explanation.

"Let me run through this for you, see if I can answer some of your questions before you ask them. I saw the envelope on my side porch Saturday and figured it was something Pauline had dropped off. I don't know how long it had been there--I don't use that side door much. That was the day you sent Rick to drive me to Ramona's. Before I left with him, I brought the envelope into the kitchen and tossed it on the counter. I didn't open it, didn't even look at it closely. When I finally opened it and realized it was from Todd Lewis, I drove it down to you." I phrased all this very carefully, making an effort to be sufficiently vague--as a former boss of mine used to say-- about the timing of these events. I also neglected to mention that I'd left the envelope with the receptionist at the center to avoid seeing him.

Jim stared at me without speaking--apparently a technique he used to get criminals to confess.

I had to admit it was an effective one. I felt compelled to stumble on. "Todd had said he was going to send me something, but I didn't realize the envelope had come from him. I thought it was from Pauline." Hadn't I just said that? He had me repeating myself already.

Jim continued to stare at me, his face set in a stiff mask.

"That's the truth," I said.

He still didn't reply.

"Jim, for God's sake, say something."

"Something that will make you feel better? How can I? If we'd known Todd had hung onto important evidence, we might have been able to catch up with him before he left the area. You understand that, don't you?" He scowled at me as if I'd personally arranged for Todd Lewis to skip town.

I nodded.

"You think the package was left on your porch, not mailed to you?"

I nodded again. "Had to be. No address, just my name."

"And when do you think it was left there?"

"I don't know. I saw it for the first time Saturday morning, but understand, I didn't know then it was from Todd."

"And you knew that when?"

"When I opened it and saw the notebook. But I didn't touch it. I dumped it out of the envelope onto the table and moved it with a pencil."

"So you looked through it." The lines around his mouth deepened as he clenched his teeth.

"Yes, I admit I turned the pages with the eraser and looked at what was written on them. Some kind of code, apparently."

"Teen stuff, probably. I've sent it to an expert in cryptography, but I suspect this cipher is pretty simple."

"I didn't touch it with my fingers so I wouldn't leave fingerprints," I assured him.

"Right now I'm more interested in exactly when this happened. When did you open it and realized it was from Todd?"

"Late Saturday, I guess. I'm not sure exactly." I was hedging now, trying to make myself look better. But it didn't matter. I was definitely in the wrong here.

"Damn it, Loren."

I didn't say anything. He rarely called me Loren. I couldn't remember when I'd seen him this angry. He was furious at me. Right now, no response was better than the wrong one.

"You found it Saturday and didn't turn it in until Monday morning. You could have at least called me."

"Look, I was wrong. I'm sorry. I had a lot to think about last weekend, remember? Deke getting shot. Ramona in such bad shape. Then Jeannie came to see me because she thought she'd insulted me by telling me to clean up Ramona's kitchen. I spent some time with her. And also--I was really faltering at that point--I had some personal concerns." I wasn't obligated to tell him about my evening with Don Morrison at the Beach House or my disagreements with Jack, was I? I was entitled to a little privacy.

"It never occurred to you time might be important?"

"No. To be honest, it didn't. Todd told me he was leaving town. I figured when I found the package he was long gone."

He sat forward in his chair, his eyes dark with anger, his face mottled under his tan.

I jumped in to divert the torrent.

"Wait. Before you blow your top, there's something more. Todd's mother gave me this yesterday afternoon. That's why I was calling you last night." I picked up the shopping bag with the pocketbook in it and dumped it out on his desk.

"Jesus, Loren. Goddamn it."

A double whammy. Actually, a triple whammy. Jim never blasphemed or cursed, and now he'd done both, on top of calling me Loren. He was pulling out all the stops on this one

"I've got a better explanation this time." I rushed ahead before he could say more. "Bella Lewis showed me the bag. I tried to get her to come with me to the Municipal Center. She absolutely refused. Said she and her husband would get a lawyer. I'm innocent on this one, I swear it. I took the pocketbook because I thought that's what you'd want me to do."

Jim puffed out his cheeks, his eyes glinting now with disbelief as he stared first at the pocketbook, then at me, then back at the pocketbook.

I flashed on the rattler coiled to strike in the motel bathroom. I slid back in my chair. Any minute now, Jim would leap across the desk and throttle me. I stumbled through my prepared script.

"There's a note there, too. Todd wrote it to send with the notebook and then decided not to."

He slipped on a pair of plastic gloves and examined the pocketbook. The initials TAS were only slightly tarnished. The leather was worn, but it certainly didn't look as if it had wintered outdoors. He still didn't speak.

I hit the high points of my story again. "Look. I'm telling you I made the right choice this time. Bella Lewis said if I refused to take it, she'd hire a lawyer. That would have held things up. Then, she handed me this note. I couldn't very well refuse to take this either."

Jim didn't respond until after he'd read the note slowly two or three times. "First, he takes the notebook, then the money. Or, maybe the other way around. How could he be so stupid? He claims he found the pocketbook, claims he had nothing to do with her death and yet he takes two things--at least he admits to two--out of it. Helps himself to valuable pieces of evidence. Of course, we're going to suspect him." He was still furious, but at least now his anger was directed at Todd Lewis instead of me.

I kept very quiet, relieved that I was no longer the primary target.

"How much money? I don't suppose you found that out in your detective work," he snarled.

"His mother insists she has no idea."

"Well, we'll see what she has to say when I talk to her."

"Jim, the woman is really upset about this. I got the feeling she was trying to do what's right."

I expected my defense of Bella Lewis to set him off again, but he held steady. Confronted with two pieces of hard evidence, he swung into efficient lawman mode. Without resorting to the intercom, he let out a bellow. "Rick. Sally. Get in here."

Rick Cronin, the deputy on duty, and Sally Winston, a secretary from the Family Court office down the hall, lost no time in responding to his summons. No one in his right mind would dawdle after hearing that roar.

I understood he was summoning them as witnesses. Jim wanted no questions later about what the pocketbook contained, no accusations that he'd added or removed anything.

He extracted a roll of heavy white paper from a drawer and tore off a piece large enough to cover the top of his desk. With a letter opener he lifted the pocketbook by its strap and set it on the paper. He motioned us closer.

"You've got pocketbooks, Sally. Does this one look like it's been exposed to the elements all winter?" he asked her.

"Well, it is real nice leather," Sally said hesitantly. "Still it doesn't seem it would hold up that well."

"Take a good long look at it and tell me everything you see." Jim's voice was calmer now.

Sally warmed to the task. "*Coach* brand. Expensive. Sell them over in Manchester. Maybe down on the Half-Mile too, but I don't know. Initials--TAS. Gold clasp. Both tarnished a little. Scratches along one side of the pocketbook. Shows some wear and tear."

Rick nodded but didn't contribute. I was smart enough to keep my mouth shut, too.

When Jim was satisfied neither of us had anything to add, he opened the clasp of the pocketbook. As we all leaned over the desk to watch, he eased the contents slowly onto an untouched section of the paper.

"Did you open this and look through it, Mayor?" He still bore an unnerving resemblance to that rattler.

"No. Absolutely not," I said, relieved that I'd done one thing right anyway.

As I stared down at the contents, I felt tears prick at my eyes. A teenager's possessions--wallet, comb, lipstick, movie ticket stub, one earring, crumbs of some kind. Of course, the notebook had been in there too. Todd had removed that; maybe he'd taken other things out as well. None of us commented as Jim unzipped two small interior compartments and slid his gloved fingers inside. Both empty.

The wallet held a plastic section containing snapshots and wallet size portraits of teenagers, both boys and girls. Tammy might have been linked to older men but she still carried school photos of her classmates. No driver's license or credit cards. Maybe the girl wouldn't have qualified for a credit card, but she must have had a license. Strange that it was missing.

Jim began calling off the items in the wallet and Sally wrote them down on her pad. Rick got his chance to contribute as they studied the photos. One by one he recognized the young people in the photographs and Sally added their names to her list.

"That's Jimmy Martin. This one's the Madison girl. That's Janie Smith."

I saw a chance to escape.

"I have to get going," I said.

My timing was perfect. Jim, caught up in studying the photos and the contents of the wallet, didn't try to stop me. I stifled a big sigh of relief as I slipped out the door.

CHAPTER TWENTY-SEVEN

NINE-THIRTY ON one of the perfect summer mornings this part of the world was famous for and I'd had enough of murder and murder evidence. I needed something else to think about. As soon as I returned to the office, I called Stephanie Colvin and picked her brain for more ideas for the Third of July Festival.

I'd caught her at a good time, she assured me, and she'd be happy to brainstorm with me.

"I think those information booths, or whatever you're going to call them, are a great idea. They'll give the festival more pizzazz and plant the idea of a community center in the public's mind too," she said.

"So what other booths could we have?" I asked her.

"You know what might work--food booths by different restaurants. You said some of the restaurant owners have jumped at the chance to serve their specialties at the Chamber meetings. Why not give them an opportunity to do it at the festival? Maybe they could charge just enough to cover the costs. It would be great advertising for them."

I seconded the idea at once. Stephanie agreed to contact several restaurant owners to get their reactions. I asked Reggie Collins if the re-enactors would make an appearance and called Don who promised the Bateaux Below group would set up a booth. Johnny Noblett agreed to display a couple of his antique boats and Matt Tremont promised to demonstrate dowsing. Plans hummed along and I was able to get through the morning without any more thoughts of Tammy Stevenson.

In the early afternoon, after Pauline had relieved me, I drove to Glens Falls, armed with my copy of the entries in Tammy's little black notebook. I went first to Crandall Library, found an idle computer in the reference section and checked for books with the subject heading *Codes*. *Codes, see Ciphers*, the database informed me. Jim had used the word, *cipher*, I remembered. Although I wasn't sure what the difference was, I complied at once. Considering the size of the library's collection of books on ciphers, it looked as if everyone in the area might be engaged in secret writing.

"Do you really have all these books?" I asked one of the librarians.

"We can get any you want through intra-library loan," she assured me. "Most of what we have will be upstairs in the Children's Room."

A few minutes later I'd gathered a pile of books and made myself comfortable on a window seat.

I saw at once I had a lot to learn. Secret messages could be written in one of two basic ways--in code or in a cipher. In a code, I read, each word had another word which stood for it. I might use the word *blue*, for example, to mean 'tomorrow', the word *cloud* to mean 'meeting.' So a message like *cloud-blue* would tell my fellow spies that our meeting would take place the next day.

Ciphers involved the substitution or transposition of letters. As I took my copy of Tammy's notations out of my pocket and studied it, I decided that was the kind of code she'd used.

Code breaking had a long and fascinating history, but I only had time to skim the surface. Fortunately for me, I had access to my own personal code breaker--Ms. Josie Donohue. The key to my success--pick her brain without giving away my game plan.

As soon as school was out, I dropped in on my young friend. A casual visit. I chatted about other things for a while, then tossed out a question.

"What's the latest on Tammy Stevenson's murder?" I asked.

"That's all anyone talks about. Now they're saying she left the name of her murderer--but it's in code."

"Really?" I bit down hard on the inside of my cheek. What I had to do was say little, let Josie do the talking. If she even suspected I'd seen Tammy's coded notes, she'd subject me to a grilling far beyond anything Investigator Thompson could dream up.

Fortunately, she was willing to tell me what she knew. "I heard they sent it to a crypto...something or other."

"A cryptographer?" I said.

"Yeah. I guess so. That's a big fat waste of time, if you ask me. Probably any of the kids could tell 'em what it said."

"And just how would they do that?"

"In health class we all used to do it. Write things in code and send messages to one another that way."

"You what?"

"We had this teacher, Mr. Pomeroy. Man, was he boring. Like he was supposed to be teaching us about sex but he couldn't handle it. So he'd give these lectures on other stuff--major snoozers. Some of us girls started sending each other messages in code just so we wouldn't fall asleep. After a while the whole class got into it."

"And Tammy was in the class? I thought she was older than you."

"She'd flunked it or something. They made her take it over. That was a laugh too, because Tammy probably knew ten times as much about sex as Mr. P. He could have made her guest lecturer and solved the problem that way."

So even the high school kids knew Tammy's reputation. But then, as I'd discovered time and again, they were often the first to know everything.

"Did Tammy get in on the coded messages?"

"Sure. Everybody did sooner or later."

"I know a little bit about writing in code. What kind did you use?" I made the remark a masterpiece of indifference, as if I really didn't care.

"We tried different ones. You can use numbers, you know. Take your ruler and write letters across the top every half inch. Then you use the number on the ruler to stand for the letter above it. But the math-challenged kids didn't like that one. So most of the time we used letters."

"Letters? I've seen letter codes, but I don't remember just what they were." I might have a future in the CIA, I was that good.

"One of the easiest ones was to write down two alphabets, one under the other. But you don't start the second one with A. You start it further on. You could change it easy--like say you started with C one time. If you thought somebody'd cracked your code, you could change it to start with another letter, like maybe H."

"Really," I said, careful not to interrupt the flow of information.

"And you know what was fun? You didn't put any spaces between the words. You'd be surprised how different words look if you run all the letters together."

Exactly what Tammy had done. The notations in her little book looked like one long word.

"Mr. P. found a note one time. Boy, was he ticked. He wanted to know what it said in the worst way, but nobody would tell him. He was really pissed."

"I'm glad I didn't become a teacher. You guys sound like a tough bunch."

"Nah. Mr. P. knew we liked him. Most of the time anyway."

I flashed on a classroom of kids passing each other coded messages while poor Mr. Pomeroy struggled with his lesson plan. It was probably easier for me to prod the Common Council toward agreement than for Mr. P. to get his students' attention. But I'd heard enough. "Did you give your mother those magazine I brought last week? If she sees any recipes she likes, maybe she'll cook one of them up for you."

"Whatever," she said and tossed me a wave as I went out.

Half an hour later I'd cleared off the desk in my den, started a pot of coffee and psyched myself for some serious code breaking. I laid out the paper on which I'd copied Tammy's notations. With Josie's instructions rattling around in my head, I rummaged through the drawers until I found a pad of lined paper and printed the alphabet along the side. An inch or two underneath, I printed the alphabet again starting with B, careful to keep the letters and the spaces between them the same size. Nothing clicked. Rather than go on printing alphabets, I cut off the bottom section of the paper in and moved it slowly along under the top strip. I kept referring to the coded words I'd copied from Tammy's notebook. Now, if Josie had set me on the right track, all I had to do was move the second alphabet under the first until something made sense.

I made one attempt after another, sliding my paper along slowly, searching for words. Gibberish. After eight or ten tries, I saw a combination of letters which could have been the start of a name. D__ E__ E__D_____. Bingo. I hurried to find the rest of the letters. DEKE DOLLY. The last name was misspelled, but it was possible that Tammy hadn't been sure of the spelling. The numbers following the name meant nothing. 50010025050. Was this another code, the one Josie had mentioned done with a ruler? Too many zeroes for that, I decided, and went on to the next item.

This time the code--from the books I'd borrowed I knew it was actually a cipher--was easy to crack. PETER FINCH. The numbers didn't make any more sense than the numbers after Deke's name. 500200300, written in several different colored inks with a line through all of them.

Could this be a record of what Tammy had earned as a chambermaid? Maybe she'd expected to clear $5.00 an hour and only received $2 or $3. But, why would she have crossed out the numbers?

ARTHUR BROWN was the next name on the list. Another motel owner. Another possible employer. Tammy had worked in several area motels. Was this a record of what she'd been paid for her work or something much more ominous? Could this have been money paid for services rendered, services other than chambermaid duties? I thought about what Jim had said--Tammy did more in motel rooms than clean them. I remembered the scene Jack had described. Had Tammy been paid for sexual encounters with men she worked for?

Confident I was on the brink of a discovery. I pressed on. I'd decipher the names first, then try to figure out what the numbers meant. The fourth name should be easy. I was a crackerjack decoder by this time.

As the letters emerged, I stared, disbelieving, at the name emerging in front of me. I flung down the pencil. Why had I done this? Why had I stuck my nose into something that was none of my business?

I pushed the paper aside. What made me think I had the right to play detective, to snoop into things which didn't concern me? I was like those women in fairy tales, women like Bluebeard's wife, who insist on searching the castle's secret rooms until they find out more than they want to know.

The fourth name on the list was JACK ROBERTS. The numbers–200300500. That sure didn't sound like a day's pay to me.

Chapter Twenty-eight

THE THIRD OF July Festival fell into place. Stephanie and I found we worked well together and her contacts and enthusiasm proved invaluable.

"Stephanie," I told her when we met to go over the final plan. "You're a wonder. I can't believe how much you've helped pull this together."

She shrugged off the compliment. "I'm sure we can expect some snafus. Some participants won't show up at all, or they'll show up and make a mess of things, but that always happens when you kick off something different. If most of the exhibitors come through for us, we should be all right."

Neither of us mentioned Jack's name. I hadn't seen or heard from him since the night he closed the door of his room in my face. Stephanie had taken over the job of chairing the committee and recruiting the restaurants.

"Great advertising for your place," she'd told the restaurant owners. "You give tourists a sample of your specialties at the festival, and your phone will be ringing off the hook afterward."

On that Friday before the festival, Stephanie and I checked and double-checked our lists one last time. We'd assigned booth space to the artists and crafts people who paid a fee for space where they could display and sell their work.

"Better than we hoped," I said when we'd completed our final tally.

"And the educational booths are all set, too," Stephanie added.

Pauline looked up from the copy machine where she was turning out maps of the grounds.

"Reggie and the re-enactors are psyched," she assured us. "And Reggie says the Bateaux Below guys are bringing samples of milfoil and zebra mussels and any other aquatic pests that swim their way before Saturday."

"The Historical Association's put together a display and Johnny Noblett is bringing two of his antique boats and a photo board showing others," I said.

Stephanie handed me a list of names. "Here are a few groups I've lined up as entertainment. This will be an area we'll want to work on another year. I've scheduled these singers and small bands to perform on the bandstand, but we could use more."

"Don't worry. If this turns out to be half as good as it looks on paper, people will be begging to take part next year," I said.

After Pauline had left for home, Stephanie and I did one last review of the map. "We've ironed out all the glitches," we assured each other.

"Thinking about those food booths has made me realize how hungry I am. I've got a meeting later, but it doesn't start until eight o'clock. Want to grab a bite to eat?" Stephanie asked me.

Fifteen minutes later Stephanie and I had settled into a booth at Mario's. For once I skipped the house specialty and ordered a Caesar salad. I gave Stephanie a chance to eat most of her individual pizza before I asked my question. "What's the latest you've heard about the Emerald Point Inn and its financial problems?"

She shook her head. "You probably know more than I do. All I've heard is that they're running in the red. Mr. Roberts had some grandiose ideas, I guess, and they've apparently backfired. At least, that's the story making the rounds."

"I knew Jack was worried, but not much more than that. That doesn't sound very good, does it?" I said.

"They'll probably pull out of it. The hotel business around here is famous for its ups and downs and this area has such short summers. Even with ski tours and leaf peepers, there are still weeks with little or no business. They say Phil Johnson is in trouble at the Point. He may be the next to go under. The hospitality business can be a house of cards."

I stabbed at my last piece of romaine. "People say that, but I've never understood why. I'd think if one place failed, there'd be that much more business for the others."

"I guess it doesn't work that way," Stephanie said. "Apparently, this kind of trouble is contagious. Like a computer virus that wipes out everybody's hard drive." She hummed a few bars of Twilight Zone music.

We both chuckled over her remark, as if nothing like that could possibly happen.

Chapter Twenty-nine

THE MORNING OF the Third of July Festival I didn't take time for breakfast. I grabbed a quick shower and shortly after six o'clock I headed for the park. The village was already awake and bathed in sunshine. At a little restaurant across from the entrance, I picked up a croissant and a large coffee to go and walked down the hill toward the lake.

We were holding the festival in our lakeside park near the center of the village. This year–if all went well–we'd be turning our small annual craft fair into a major event. I breathed a sigh of relief when I saw the first influx of exhibitors arriving and setting up their booths. Although it was still early, people were bustling about, unloading vans and pickups next to their assigned spots.

Armed with one of the maps of the grounds, I began directing new arrivals to their places and handing out the color coded packets we'd prepared for our exhibitors. Stephanie and Pauline arrived a few minutes later and pitched in to help.

The three of us divided the list of participants and walked about greeting the exhibitors. The layout of the park suited our purposes. Several narrow blacktopped walks ran parallel to the lake, the first one just below the crest of the hill. The flat space on both sides was wide enough for booths. Veterans of the craft fair circuit were already at work, erecting the white pop-up tents called E-Z Ups and arranging their merchandise. The novices, trusting to good weather, had brought collapsible tables on which to display their wares.

In less than an hour almost all the two dozen vendors who'd signed up had laid out the items they wanted to sell–jewelry, folk art, macramé hangings, pottery, pillows, housewares, paintings–just about everything you could think of. A husband and wife team who'd paid for an extra large space were displaying decorative wooden objects–cutting boards, lawn ornaments, garden sticks, even birdhouses which–their sign announced–could be special ordered to match your house.

"Look at these," I called to Stephanie who was talking to the exhibitors at another booth. "I should hang one of these on my lamp post."

"You can order it right now," the woman assured me, giving me her business card. "All we need is a photograph and we can have it for you in a couple of weeks."

Her can-do attitude proved to be typical of most of the vendors I talked to.

"Good luck," I said to another woman who was hanging up handmade aprons and smocks.

"Oh, I'll sell most of these without any trouble. I always do. Nurses like the smocks and everybody loves to find a pretty apron. Most of the factory-mades nowadays are so ugly they'd make a soufflé fall."

I stopped by the Bateaux Below booth where Don Morrison was displaying an aquarium stocked with zebra mussels. He'd already attracted a group of youngsters to watch his demonstration of how the zebra mussels attached themselves to docks and boats. Reggie Collins, dressed in full battle regalia, was greeting new arrivals and handing out maps of historic sites.

By the time the three of us had finished our visits to the booths on the upper level, a second road farther down the hill was swarming with activity. Representatives from the participating restaurants and civic organizations were carrying the park's picnic tables into a grassy area in the center, setting up an outdoor food court convenient to all the booths.

As I descended the hill, I smelled the enticing aroma of coffee and cinnamon buns emanating from Nora's Bakery booth. Nearby, the local Chamber of Commerce members were hard at work, deep-frying their signature bread dough. "Fry bread" they called it in the Southwest, *galettes* in some cultures, but fabulous tasting no matter what the name or shape. Mario's booth was already serving a variety of pizzas. The gang clamoring for slices confirmed Don's belief that Mario's pizzas were as delicious for breakfast as they were any other time.

At twelve o'clock, with a steady stream of visitors circulating among the booths, I found an empty picnic table and sat down. I surveyed the food area, considering the choices for lunch.

Stephanie slipped onto the bench next to me. "Could we have asked for a more beautiful day?"

She was right. We'd been favored with perfect weather. Warm and sunny, but not so hot people would be running for their air-conditioned cars after a half-hour stay. Lake George never gave any guarantees, I'd discovered, but most years the area managed enough of these fabulous summer days to keep both tourists and locals satisfied.

The food court was filling up. The participating restaurants put their best foot forward by featuring their specialties. The Beach House on the Point had set up a seafood booth, with Phil Johnson himself commanding the young workers he'd brought along to open clams and oysters. As the lines in front of the booth lengthened, Tom Bailey pitched in to help. Jeannie Spenser turned up to order an assortment of seafood and chat for a while with Phil and Tom. One spot remained noticeably empty–the section we'd designated for the Emerald Point Inn.

Stephanie sensed what I was thinking. "Looks like Jack's a no-show, Loren. He didn't even bother to call back to say he wasn't coming."

I didn't comment. I'd resolved not to let Jack's defection bother me.

Pauline joined us at the table. "I ran into Reggie a few minutes ago. He's already sold a dozen or more of those battle maps the re-enactors printed up for today, but I'm afraid he's getting overheated in that heavy uniform. I'm going to buy him some lunch and take it over to him," she said.

Don Morrison wandered toward us. "Looks like you've got a successful event going here, ladies. Tell me something I can do to help and I'll do it."

His presence sent pheromones swarming through the air. Stephanie raised her eyebrows at me in a questioning glance. Obviously, Don and I were becoming an item, whether I wanted it or not. Still, I could hardly tell him to go away.

"I think we're okay right now," I said.

"Let me do something. Want anybody roughed up or thrown out? Not that I'm implying you couldn't handle that yourselves if you had a mind to, but I'll be glad to step in and save you the trouble." He flashed an infectious smile.

"Thanks anyway, but I think we're okay."

"So, does that mean I don't get an assignment?" Don said.

I stood up, shaking my head. "Right now, I want to make another round of the booths. You can have this table if you're going to eat."

Stephanie shot me a look which asked why I was putting Don off. The answer was simple enough--I enjoyed his company but I wasn't ready to start tongues wagging any more by wandering the grounds with him.

"Well, somebody's handling my booth for the afternoon. So if you don't have anything for me to do, I might as well take off." He sounded hurt, but I didn't relent.

The feeling of disappointment I felt as he walked away caught me by surprise. Stephanie and I made another tour of the booths and met back at the food court later in the afternoon. As we sat down with a cold drink, I noticed a group of high school kids who'd taken over the stage of the band shell.

The young band members bustled around, setting up their instruments and music stands, obviously delighted at the chance to perform. A crowd of teenagers drifted down the hill. Todd Lewis's parents, canvas chairs slung over their shoulders, joined them, positioning themselves near the bandstand. Why would they be here, I wondered? One of the guitar players, a baseball cap pulled low over his forehead, tucked his chin into his chest and slipped into a chair behind the other band members. As he started to tune up, I tried to make out his features under the cap.

The sky darkened. A shadow fell across the bandstand and covered the lower edge of the park. An ominous crack of thunder echoed from beyond Tongue Mountain.

Pauline hurried over to where we were standing. "This is going to be a bad one. People are starting to leave."

Gusts of wind scurried through the park. The shadow crept up the hill toward us, staining the ground with its dark penumbra.

"Good thing it's almost closing time," I said.

The exhibitors, anxious to get out before the rain hit, were packing up their merchandise and dismantling canopies at breakneck speed. People dashed for their vehicles and jockeyed them close to their booths. Reggie, still in his uniform, hurried over to one of the booths and began hauling boxes up the hill to a van.

"He's helping some friends of ours. I'd better give them a hand too," Pauline said.

"Maybe we should pitch in ourselves," Stephanie and I said at the same time and ran to the nearest booth.

"Here, we can do that," I told two women struggling with their E-Z Up. Stephanie and I collapsed it like a giant umbrella. Relieved, the women turned their attention to their leftover pillows and bedding, grabbing unsold items off the counter and stuffing them into plastic bags.

The storm swooped down on us. Black clouds raced over the mountains bringing more wind and the first spattering of rain. The musicians packed their instruments; the audience at the bandstand scattered. The boy in the baseball cap, carrying his guitar, approached Mr. and Mrs. Lewis. He leaned forward quickly and kissed Mrs. Lewis on the cheek. Todd. It had to be Todd. He unchained a bike from one of the benches and slung his guitar case over his back.

"Wait," Mrs. Lewis called after him.

Mr. Lewis unlocked a car parked on the edge of the road. Both the Lewis's climbed in; the boy biked across the grass to the car. He slid his guitar into the back seat, then climbed in himself, flinging the bike down behind him on the grass. The bike was a mountain bike, the one Todd had been riding the first time I saw him.

"That's Todd Lewis," I said to Stephanie as we took refuge in her car. "I'd love a chance to talk to him alone, but I don't want to freak him out."

We huddled in the car as the rain pelted the roof and windshield. A calamity like this separated the experienced exhibitors from the newbies. Most of the regulars on the fair circuit had managed to pack up their merchandise and get it into their vans before the storm hit. Those who hadn't moved quickly enough waited in their vehicles for a chance to dismantle their booths.

A break in the storm produced a flurry of activity. People jumped from their vans and, slipping and sliding, rushed to pack whatever they'd left behind.

Todd Lewis pushed the door of his parents' car open and got out. When his mother rolled down her window, he leaned in and kissed her again on the cheek. She reached up her hand and touched his face in a loving gesture.

Todd shook his bike back and forth, sending a shower of raindrops in all directions, and pedaled up the road toward the highway. When he reached the exit, he hung a right and disappeared from sight.

"Stephanie, I want to talk to this kid. I'll meet you at Mario's."

I slid out of her van and ran for my car. I made it up the hill in seconds, only to find a steady stream of traffic moving along the highway. Two cars ahead of me had their blinkers on to turn left and there was no way around them. By the time I caught a break and got out of the park, Todd was long gone.

CHAPTER THIRTY.

I DROVE NORTH, scanning the edges of the highway for places Todd might have turned in, but I couldn't guess which of the narrow, tree-lined roads he might have chosen. I passed the road which led to the Beach House on the Point. Unless Todd had a job there–and that seemed unlikely--he couldn't afford to stay at a prime lakefront location like that. When I came on the entrance to the campsites, I felt I was getting warmer. If Todd pitched a tent there, he could hold down a job somewhere close by and still remain out of sight.

I took one of the dirt roads which wound down the hill toward the lake. Campers were emerging from tents and trailers to begin tidying up after the storm. People brushed water from outdoor chairs and awnings, wiped off picnic tables, swept twigs and branches away from their campsites. When I reached the lake, I swung the car around in a wide turn and tried another road. A few sites down I saw Todd Lewis's bike chained to a tree in front of a small, weather-worn tent.

I left my car on the road and approached the site cautiously, anxious not to scare Todd off. When I'd planted myself firmly outside the closed flap of the tent, I called his name in low voice. "Todd, Todd Lewis. Can you come out a minute?"

Todd fumbled with the flap, then stuck his head out. "Jeez. What the hell are you doin' here?" He glanced wildly around, checking to see if anyone was with me.

"Wait. I just want to ask you a couple questions. This is important, Todd."

"What the hell are you doing here?" he said again. He looked sickly pale beneath his tan.

"Calm down. I saw you at the park. I just need to talk to you."

"Damn it. I shouldn't have done that gig. I told the guys I shouldn't do it, but I let 'em talk me into it. You're gonna rat on me to the sheriff's office, tell them where I am."

I didn't want him to bolt, but I told the truth. "Actually, I want you to turn yourself in. It's time, you know. You can't stay here forever."

"Forget it. No way I'm gonna do that."

"Todd, I've been to your house. Your mother gave me Tammy's pocketbook. I've given that and her notebook to the sheriff's investigator. You need to tell him anything you know about what happened to her."

"Sure. So they can decide I killed her and lock me up."

"I don't think they'll do that. Anyway, how long can you stay here?"

"I'm not turning myself in," he insisted.

I glanced around the site, appalled at its limitations. "Todd, you have nothing—a tent and maybe a sleeping bag inside. I don't even see a grill or a fireplace to cook on."

"Yeah, it's pretty bad here. I should get out of this place, go somewhere else, but my parents don't want me to. They won't give me the money to take off and I don't have anything left myself."

"What do your parents want you to do?"

"Like you said, turn myself in and get this thing settled. But I can't, I just can't do it. They'll blame me. I know they will."

"Can we sit down a minute and talk about this? Maybe I can help you think of something." I pointed him toward a rickety picnic table a few yards from the tent.

To my surprise, he walked over to the table and sat down. I settled myself across from him. "Todd, tell me the truth. Do you know who killed Tammy? Is that why you're hiding?" What I really wanted to know was if he had killed her himself, but I didn't expect him to tell me that.

He appeared disgusted by my question. "Of course not. I wouldn't hang around here if I knew who did it, take a chance on them killing me, too. I'm not that stupid."

"Let's talk about what you do know. I want to help you, but I need to understand You realized the car was Tammy's, right?"

He shifted on the hard bench of the picnic table. He wiped a hand across his face, streaking dirt over his cheeks, the same gesture his mother had made in her garden. His mouth opened and closed as if words were fighting to escape, but he made no sound.

I waited. I gave him time to make up his mind.

When the words came, they streamed out in a rush. "I was with Tammy at Vic's. We were friends–that's all we ever were."

"Friends?"

"Friends. I'm tellin' you the truth. Tammy wouldn't have sex with me. She did it with other guys. At least, that's what kids in school said. But she and I had been friends since seventh grade and she never let me kiss her, touch her, anything."

The confession surprised me. "Did she tell you why she wouldn't?"

"She claimed I was her friend and she wanted to keep it that way. Said I was special, that she knew I liked her for herself, not like the guys who were just after her for sex."

"And you did--like her for herself, I mean?"

"Hell, if you gotta know, I more than liked her. I was crazy about her. I couldn't stand to think of her doing those jerks and then not lettin' me near her."

Hadn't he just given me a perfect motive for murder? I shivered, suddenly aware of a cold wind blowing out of the pines. The storm was over, the temperature dropping fast as it often did here at the lake. "So what happened that night at Vic's?"

"We were sitting together in a booth. All of a sudden she jumped up and ran out. Saw somebody on the patio, I guess. She barreled right out of there without a word to me. Left her pocketbook in the booth even. I figured she'd be back. I sat there waiting like a damn fool."

"She left the pocketbook then? But you said you found it near where you found the car."

"I couldn't very well admit I'd had it for a year."

"You had it all that time and Tammy never came back for it?"

His face twisted as if he were in pain. "No, that's what I'm telling you. That's the last time I saw her."

"So what did you do then?"

"I put the pocketbook under my jacket so nobody'd see me carrying it and went out to look for her. Her car was gone from the parking lot. She must have had her keys in her jacket. So I went home. I figured she'd call me about it, but she never did."

I didn't know whether to believe him or not. "But, when you knew she was missing, why didn't you go to the sheriff and report all this? Maybe you could have helped them find her. "

"I didn't dare. I was afraid they'd accuse me of something. Tell me you're not sitting here right now, figuring I'm making this all up."

He was right. Todd might be naïve, but he wasn't stupid. If I found loopholes in his story–and I'd spotted some big ones--Jim would find even more.

I switched directions. "So the last time you saw Tammy, you took the pocketbook home and hid it. Was there money in it?"

He looked away. I could see his cheeks redden. I'd hit a nerve.

We sat a minute in uncomfortable silence before he said, "Yeah, a couple hundred bucks. I ended up spending it. I swear I meant to pay it back. But when I got caught short and I knew it was right there, I dipped into it."

"But her license? Did you do something with that? Wasn't that in her wallet, too?"

"No she usually kept that in her pocket, along with her fake I.D in case she got proofed."

"But how did you know where the car was? That day I found you on the trail, you knew the car was in the lake."

"I'd been searching for it. I figured at first she'd run off some place, but when nobody heard from her, I got worried. I kept lookin' around the lake. Not during the winter. I couldn't do much then. Once the snow went, I started up again. I found the car just before you got there that day. I was afraid to say I'd been looking for it, afraid it would seem like I'd known where it was all along." His voice tapered off.

"What about her body? You must have seen that, too, hadn't you?"

"No, I swear I didn't know she was there. I swear it. I saw the car was empty. I thought first maybe she'd dumped it and taken off. Then I got thinking she might have climbed out somehow and drowned or that her body had floated away. The windows were all open, remember?"

"Todd, listen to me. I want you to turn yourself in right now. Your parents are right. The longer you hide out, the guiltier you look. I'll try to help you if you're straight with me. They may not arrest you if you go to the sheriff yourself. But if somebody finds you hiding out, it's going to be a whole different story."

I studied his face as he tried to make up his mind. He'd lied about the pocketbook. How could I believe he was telling the truth now? I remembered Matt Tremont saying that things shifted around under the water. Todd probably knew that happened, too. He'd lived around here all his life. He could have believed Tammy's body floated away.

"So will you do it? Will you go with me to the sheriff's office?" When he didn't answer, I said, "Okay, come on. Let's do it. Let's start down there right now. We can talk more on the way."

"Can I bring my bike?"

A good sign. I waited while he unlocked the chain holding his bike to the tree and slid it into the back seat. Didn't this kid have anything else of value or did he assume he'd be back to the tent before night? I couldn't decide if I felt relief or guilt as I pulled out of the campsite and headed toward the Northway.

Todd squirmed in the seat, nervous about his decision. As we passed a gas station with an outside phone, he blurted out, "I gotta stop and call my parents, tell them what I'm doin.'"

Or maybe make his escape. I pulled out my cell phone. "What's their number? This will save time."

He gave me the number and let me call. I told his mother who I was and handed the phone over to him. He mumbled an explanation in such a low voice that, even sitting next to him, I could scarcely make out what he was saying.

"She and my dad will meet us at the sheriff's office. She's calling a lawyer," he said as he handed me back the phone.

"Good idea. You should have help with this."

This is almost too easy, I thought as we exited the Northway near the Municipal Center. Of course, I was right.

Chapter Thirty-one

As I turned into the Center driveway, Todd exploded. "Wait, stop. I've changed my mind. I can't do this."

I slowed the car but I didn't stop. "What's the matter? You don't want to back out now, do you?"

"My watch. I've left my watch in the tent."

"Your watch? That's what you're worrying about?"

"It was my grandfather's. I can't leave it there."

I kept going, following the road we were on to the rear of the Center where the sheriff's department was located.

"You've got to take me back to my campsite."

I eased the car toward an empty parking place.

"My grandfather's watch. Damn it. I propped it up next to me 'cause I was gonna sleep for a while and I never picked it up. My parents will kill me if I lose it."

I considered reminding him his parents were probably ready to kill him anyway, but I thought better of it. "Hold on a minute. Let's think about this. Maybe I can get it for you somehow."

He was still protesting when Mrs. Lewis and a man I assumed was Todd's father pulled into the parking lot. Their arrival provided the break I needed.

"You've got to go through with this now. I'll find a way to get your watch," I told him.

As Todd's parents crossed the parking lot toward us, Jim appeared in the door of the sheriff's department. He glowered as the four of us walked toward him. I didn't blame him. We were a scraggly little group. Mrs. Lewis, her face lined with worry, hadn't taken time to freshen up or comb her hair. Todd's dad looked like a man who'd been ripped from his Saturday chores and Todd, even in dry clothes, was dirty and disheveled. I wouldn't have won any prizes myself.

Jim, of course, was immaculately groomed, his blazer and slacks crisp and pressed even at the end of a long day.

"Come in, Todd, Mr. and Mrs. Lewis," he said in his most official tone.

My name didn't make the cut. Instead of an invitation inside, I earned an angry scowl and a very clear signal to "get lost."

Fine. I could take a hint. I whispered to Todd as he walked away. "I'll get the watch for you. Don't worry about it."

I turned my car around and headed back north, cursing myself all the way. I wanted to meet up with Stephanie, review the day's events over wine and dinner, compare notes on the fair while everything was fresh in our minds. Damn kid. Damn me and my big mouth.

By the time I pulled into the campground, another storm was threatening. The sun had disappeared and shadows in ominous shapes were creeping out from under the trees. The campers I'd seen cleaning up their sites that afternoon had disappeared. Maybe the downpour had scared them off or–well, after all, it was Saturday night–sent them out for dinner and a movie.

As I parked in front of Todd's tent, I heard voices. Through the trees I could see Tom Bailey–at least I thought it was Tom–talking with someone I didn't recognize. The two of them had set up a tripod and were taking measurements with surveying equipment. Strange. But I didn't take time to speculate about it.

I dug through my glove compartment for my little flashlight and walked over to the tent. I pushed aside the flap. The smell of sweat and unwashed clothing sent waves of nausea sweeping over me. Why hadn't I asked Todd where he'd left the watch? I shuddered at the thought of pawing through the tattered sleeping bag and the pile of dirty shirts and jeans.

Hoping for an easy way out, I opened a small metal box which looked like a good hiding place for valuables. Nothing except odds and ends of food. The box may have kept the food safe from woodland creatures, but its odor was even more disgusting than the one permeating the tent. Get the watch, I told myself, then you can call Stephanie and make dinner plans–providing you can still get food down.

Once I'd accepted the fact I wasn't going to find a shortcut, I began to search systematically, shaking out the blanket and articles of clothing and setting them aside. Finally, I glimpsed what looked like the band of a watch inside a sneaker, a foul-smelling, disgusting sneaker ready for the garbage dump. I ignored my qualms and shoved my fingers deep into the toe. I extracted the watch and slipped it into my pocket.

Eager for a breath of fresh air, I lifted the flap and stepped outside. Immediately, something grabbed me from behind. I thought first of a bear. I'd heard stories of bears at campsites, not here at Emerald Point, but a few miles farther north--bears drawn by food carelessly stored or garbage left strewn about. Todd's tent smelled bad enough to bring a bear all the way from the Arctic circle. My heart pounded in my chest. I tried to pull away, but I couldn't move.

Whatever was holding me wasn't a bear. Muscular arms pinned my arms to my side. A blanket of some kind was thrown over my head. I twisted, desperate to escape. I kicked back, hoping to connect with my attacker, but he'd imprisoned me in a vise. I struggled to loosen the arms wrapped around me. It was no use. I felt myself forced to the ground, shoved face down in the dirt. A knee dug into the small of my back; a hand rammed into a pocket of my slacks, yanked out the contents, then shoved deep into the other pocket. Everything in both pockets was ripped out–a tissue, my car keys, Todd's watch. Why? I'd left my pocketbook in my unlocked car. It was easy to spot, right there on the front seat and I had money in my wallet. Was Todd's grandfather's watch so valuable that someone would attack me for it?

The weight on me shifted a little. I made another attempt to get away. A fist slammed against the side of my head. The blow stung; my eyes watered. The ringing in my ears shut out any other sounds, but in a few seconds I felt the knee taken out of my back, the weight lifted from my body.

Good deeds be dammed. I lay flat in the dirt outside Todd Lewis's tent and tried to figure out how to get to my feet. So many parts of my body ached I couldn't decide which hurt the most–my head where I'd been hit, my legs stinging from their contact with the hard ground, the small of my back where the knee had ground into it. I sent messages to my muscles to get me out of there, but they ignored me. An eternity ticked by before I managed to roll over onto my back and sit up.

Whoever had jumped me had run off, but for all I knew he could come rushing back any minute to finish the job. I forced my right arm out away from my body and groped along the ground for my car keys. I'd heard them hit when he flung them away. Dusk had settled over the campground; total darkness was only a few minutes off. I fumbled along the ground. I kept another key in my pocketbook, but the thief had probably taken that.

Still in a sitting position, I worked my way along the ground. I saw the watch first, saw it as a thin shaft of light gleaming against the dark earth. Miraculously, my keys and flashlight had landed only a few inches away. I shoved the watch into my pocket and reached for the keys. I held the flashlight in front of me like a weapon as I got to my feet.

I stumbled to my car and climbed in. I made sure I locked the doors, then I turned on the dome light. My pocketbook lay upside down on the passenger side; its contents spilled across the seat and onto the floor. I picked up my wallet but I didn't stop to check the money. I could see my license and credit cards in their plastic compartments–that was good enough.

I took a couple of slow, deep breaths and drove to the park entrance. An attendant, probably not more than sixteen, hung out the window of the small wooden booth, sweet-talking a group of teenage girls.

"I need your help. Call 911 for me. Someone just attacked me at a campsite over there," I told him.

His smile vanished. He was all business as he reached for the phone.

While he was calling in the report, I turned to the girls. "Be careful. Stay here and stay together. I just ran into some trouble."

"Where?" one girl asked. She and her friends huddled close to the booth.

"Better wait here until a deputy can take you back to your campsite," I said.

The young attendant–Jay Morrell, according to his name tag–put in a second call, this one to the park ranger. "Are you all right? Don't you want to come into the booth and sit down?" he asked me.

I shook my head. "I'd rather wait in the car. But don't let these girls leave. They're safer here than they would be on the road."

As soon as I was back in my car with the doors locked, I examined my wallet. No money missing, everything present and accounted for. Strange.

A few minutes later, Rick Cronin, the deputy on duty, responded to the call. "Mayor, are you saying that he searched your pockets, went through the stuff in your car, then didn't take anything. He must have been looking for something specific."

The teenage girls clustered around his car, twittering like a flock of birds at nightfall who couldn't find their way home.

"Our parents are going to wonder what's happened to us. We said we'd come right back," one said.

"Maybe I'd better give these girls a ride to their campsite before I finish taking your statement," Rick said. "Stay in your car, Mayor Graham, and keep the doors locked. I'll call this in and see if there've been other reports of attacks this evening."

"I'll go through my pocketbook again while you're gone," I told him.

I made a second, more careful search of my pocketbook and wallet. Money, credit cards, everything there. I even found the silver pen I carried more as a good luck charm than a writing implement still nestled at the bottom.

Apparently, my attacker had been searching for something specific. I was afraid I knew what it was.

CHAPTER THIRTY-TWO

I'D NEVER WASTED any time wanting a rescuer or any sympathy on women who did, but when Don Morrison pulled up to the park ranger's kiosk at the entrance to the campground that Saturday night, I felt a ton of weight go flying off my shoulders.

"Loren, what the hell happened?" he said as he rushed toward me. "Stephanie and I were waiting for you at Mario's when somebody heard on a scanner you'd been attacked." He opened the car door, reached in to put his arms around me.

Right then, I didn't care if the whole town saw us. I leaned my head gratefully on his shoulder. "I drove up to get Todd Lewis's watch for him and somebody jumped me," I said.

"At the campsite? Do you have any idea why? Are you hurt?" He massaged my shoulders gently as his questions poured over me.

"I got knocked in the head, but I'm all right. I'm not sure why somebody attacked me. He searched my pocketbook but didn't take the money out of my wallet. It would have been easy enough to do that; it was right there." I started to tell him about Tammy Stevenson's notebook, the one thing I thought might explain the attack, but it seemed like too much trouble. My head was aching in earnest now.

"What time is it anyway? I'm starving," I said instead.

"You need to get out of here. Rick Cronin just drove up. Let me see if I can hurry him along with whatever he needs to do about this."

Rick was quick to oblige. "I can write this up all right, Mayor, with what you've told me. Then I'll keep checking around to see if anybody else was attacked or if campers around there saw or heard anything suspicious. I'll call you tomorrow and let you know what I find out."

Don slipped farther into take-charge mode.

147

"I'll drive her home then," he told Rick. "I don't think she should drive herself. She can leave her car here, can't she?"

"Sure. I'll get somebody to bring it down to her house sometime tonight. No problem," Rick said.

I thanked him and handed him the keys.

"Stephanie's having a fit," Don said after he'd helped me into his car and pulled out onto the highway. "Do you mind if we stop at Mario's and let her know you're all right? She was dying to come with me, but I wasn't sure you'd want the press around."

"Mario's sounds good. I need a drink and something to eat," I said.

"Forget the drink. Food's okay, but alcohol after a blow to the head. Don't even think about it."

That's the trouble with rescuers. They get bossy.

Stephanie was waiting for us in Mario's back booth. "Loren, are you all right? He wouldn't let me come with him. Sit down and tell me everything."

Over Don's objections, I ordered a glass of wine along with a bowl of New England clam chowder. "One will counteract the other," I assured him, then filled Stephanie in on what had happened at the campsite.

She heard me out without interrupting. When I'd finished, she said, "Somebody was looking for something. That's obvious. Do you know what it could have been?"

I hesitated, then told her and Don about Tammy Stevenson's notebook and the copy I'd made of her coded jottings.

"I think the guy was looking for either the notebook or the copy I'd made of what was in it. He must have suspected I still had it or that I'd kept a copy. He wasn't after money or credit cards and I can't think of anything else he could have been looking for."

"But if Todd hung onto the notebook all this time, why hadn't whoever was after it tried to get it from him?" Stephanie asked.

"Beats me. Unless nobody knew he had it. You know, I did borrow some books on codes and ciphers from the library a couple of days ago. Maybe somebody saw me signing them out. Or maybe Todd told someone about sending the notebook to me." There had to be other possibilities, but my brain was too fuzzy to come up with them. Don had been right. The wine wasn't a good idea. My head buzzed with noise and my voice sounded as if it were echoing down a long tunnel.

Don gave me an appraising look. "I'd better get you home. Finish the rest of that soup, why don't you, and we'll get going," he said.

Bossy or not, he was right. This time I didn't argue with him.

BY THE TIME we reached my house, I was fighting to stay awake. Don parked as close as he could get to the back door and came around to help me out of the car. He slid an arm around my waist and I leaned heavily against him, not at all sure I could walk to the door on my own.

I handed him the key and he unlocked the kitchen door. As he switched on the overhead light, I let out a surprised gasp. The kitchen was in shambles, drawers open, papers tossed around on counters and floor.

"Somebody's been in here." I wasn't too fuzzy to make that observation.

"And maybe is still here." Don whisked me out the door, reaching for his cell phone to dial 911. "Let's sit in my car until the deputy gets here just in case." He shepherded me back to the car and settled me in the front seat.

Rick Cronin allowed himself a sharp grunt of surprise when he arrived on the scene a few minutes later.

"You're making me earn my pay tonight, Mayor Graham. Somebody's sure got it in for you."

Rick insisted Don and I wait in the car while he checked the house. "Only the kitchen's involved," he said when he returned. "If your burglar was looking for something specific–and I'd have to assume he was–he must have found it. He apparently didn't need to look any further."

"I made it easy for him, I guess." As we walked back inside, I told Rick how I'd copied the entries in Tammy's notebook. "I even left the code and cipher books I borrowed from the library on the counter. Not that he needed them. I'd deciphered most of the coded writing and left a copy of it on top of the books."

Rick scratched his head. "I don't get this. Are you talking about the notebook you turned into Jim?"

"Yes, but I kept a copy of what Tammy wrote and it's gone. That must be what the burglar was after," I said.

"Uh oh. Jim's not going to like this. Were you trying to figure out the code yourself?" he asked.

"I did figure it out. At least some of it. Here I'll show you what it said." I tore a sheet of paper off the telephone pad and wrote the names Tammy had recorded. I felt like a traitor when I came to Jack's name, but I included it anyway. I'd gotten myself in enough trouble playing code breaker. No sense making matters worse with half-truths.

Don and Rick stood on opposite sides of me, looking over my shoulders. I turned around to see them exchanging surprised glances.

"Are you sure you deciphered these correctly?" Rick asked.

"I didn't get the fifth name and I'm not sure what the numbers mean, but I think these are the names of men Tammy was getting money from. The figures probably stand for the amount of money she got. She might have been getting it over a period of time."

Don clamped his jaws tight and didn't comment.

Rick held the piece of paper out in front of him as if expecting it to flare up in spontaneous combustion. "Jim's on his way over. He's not going to like this. Not at all."

"To hell with Jim. I can't stay awake one minute longer. Lock the door when you leave."

Rick's big brown eyes expanded to saucer size. "Maybe you should hold off until he gets here, Mayor. I think he'll bring a fingerprint guy with him. This isn't a simple burglary. Looks like somebody wants to know what's in that notebook, wants to know bad enough to search Todd's tent, your car and now your house to find out."

Don finally allowed himself a comment. "You turned the notebook in, Loren, but somebody still came here looking for it?"

"Either the perp didn't hear she turned it in, or it's somebody knows the mayor well enough to figure she'd keep a copy," Rick said.

"I'll vote for answer number two," I told him, "since it's impossible to keep a secret about anything in this town. Tell Jim if he wants to bawl me out again, he can do it tomorrow. Rick, leave me a note saying if it's all right to clean up this mess. Don, thanks for all your help. I'm going to bed."

While Rick stammered out another attempt to dissuade me, I swept out of the kitchen into the hall. At least I tried to sweep. My exit was ruined when I staggered against the wall and almost fell, but I grabbed the banister, pulled myself up the stairs and collapsed into bed.

CHAPTER THIRTY-THREE

THE NEXT MORNING when I limped downstairs rubbing my aching head, most of the mess had been tidied up. The cryptology books--all present and accounted for--were stacked on the counter. Someone had added the jottings I'd made for Rick and Don to the pile, but my original decoding notes had disappeared. The contents of my junk drawer, which had been scattered over the floor, now lay in neat rows along the counter. Junk drawers weren't supposed to be neat, at least in my mind, so I swept the leftover odds and ends back into the drawer while I waited for my coffee.

By the time I'd downed my requisite two cups and toasted an English muffin, I felt almost human. I showered and slipped on a pair of dressy navy slacks and a neat blue polo shirt. I thought of calling Don to thank him, but if he'd hung around last night picking up the kitchen after the sheriff's deputies finished their work, he was probably still sleeping.

Even after my caffeine fix, my thinking was muddled. I remembered something about Tom Bailey. I'd seen him at the campgrounds, hadn't I? I just hadn't paid much attention. What was he doing there, and was it only coincidence he happened to be at the campground shortly before I was attacked? But Tom had no reason to be searching for the notebook or the copy I'd made of Tammy's blackmail account--unless, I realized finally, his was the fifth name, the one I hadn't decoded.

My aches and pains might have subsided, but I still wasn't thinking clearly. You run enough meetings, I told myself. Do what you do at them--make yourself an agenda and have at it. Not a bad idea. I'd start with old business, clear that up, then move on to the new. I found the Lewis family's number. Bella answered the phone.

"How did it go with Investigator Thompson yesterday?" I asked.

"I planned to call you as soon as I was sure you'd be up, Loren. We can't thank you enough for getting Todd to turn himself in. Jim put him through a pretty tough session, scared him half to death and his dad and me, too, to tell the truth."

"You were glad you had your lawyer there, I bet."

"Jim was trying to impress on Todd that he should have turned the pocketbook in a long time ago. I can't fault him for that. They think the little notebook may give them a clue to who killed Tammy."

"So, are they going to charge Todd with anything?"

"He isn't out of the woods yet, but at least he's back home. And we have you to thank for it."

"Tell him I have his watch," I said and left it like that. I didn't mention the attack at the campgrounds or the break-in at my house. Todd and his parents would find out soon enough that hanging on to Tammy's notebook for a year could have meant far more serious consequences than any of them yet realized.

Getting Todd to turn himself in had been the right thing to do. I felt good about it, so good I decided to tackle the big guy himself.

My opening line had worked well with Bella Lewis. I used it again when Jim Thompson picked up the phone. "So how did it go with the Lewis family yesterday?"

"All right. I was at your house last night, but they told me you'd gone to bed."

If he was waiting for an apology, he'd have a long wait. "They got that right. I was too beat to wait up for you. Being a crime victim twice in one evening does that to a person."

"Jumped and burglarized all within a few hours, I understand. Any reason for it that you know of?"

"The price of playing amateur cryptologist, I suppose."

"Yeah. I saw the stuff you jotted down for Rick. We were working on that, you know. You could have waited."

I didn't want to argue the point. I had bigger fish to fry. "Jim, what I don't understand–why did it matter that I kept a copy? Didn't whoever was looking for it know I'd turned it in to the department?"

"I suppose he or they–maybe we should say they–wanted to know the contents of that notebook right away. Another possibility, of course, is that someone thought there was more in the notebook than there actually was."

I'd spent time deciphering what I'd found in the notebook, but I hadn't thought much about what hadn't been in it. Points off my detecting score.

"You mean they thought there might be more details, more incriminating evidence?"

"Somebody wanted to know bad enough to break into Tammy's glove compartment at the garage, then go to Todd's tent and your house. It's possible your young friend tore out pages with additional facts and figures on them. He swears he didn't, but we're going check with a few stores–see if we can determine how many pages were in the book originally."

I hadn't thought about that either, but I didn't have to admit it.

"Do you think you'll be charging Todd with anything?"

"If I arrested people for stupidity, the jail would be full."

If that crack was meant for me, it was subtle enough to ignore.

"One more thing–do you know for sure what the numbers mean? Were they the amounts Tammy asked as blackmail?"

"Most likely. Asked or got, or both. For example, she may have asked for $500, then agreed to take it in smaller amounts. That would explain that 500300200. Remember how some of the numbers were crossed out? Looks like she offered an easy payment plan for her silence."

"You have this pretty well figured out, I guess."

"My job. In fact, it might be a good idea if we both stuck to our own jobs from now on."

That one was definitely meant for me. No subtlety there, but I was glad to be let off so easily. "Not a problem," I said and hung up.

I was willing to stick to my own job, but that didn't mean I couldn't ask questions of friends. I decided to start with Ramona.

Jeannie opened her side door in response to my knock.

"Mother's in the den. She's not receiving guests, but she'll want to see you," she said.

"I don't want to bother her."

"No, no. She'll be so pleased you've come." She stepped back and motioned me inside.

I'd expected to see Ramona huddled in a chair as beaten down and disheveled as she'd been the last time I saw her. Instead, I found her neatly dressed and well-groomed, not merely her old self, but a neater, more presentable self than I'd seen in some time.

"It's so good of you to come, Loren. He died around midnight, I guess. They called me a short time later. I'm sorry I wasn't with him when he passed, but they said he slipped away peacefully."

I stared at her blankly. Deke was dead and she thought I knew it, assumed that was why I'd come.

"I can't wish him back, not the way he was these last few days." She rambled on with more details about the call she'd received from the hospital the night before.

Jeannie had remained standing in the doorway of the den.

"Come into the kitchen, Loren. I've got fresh coffee. Mother doesn't want to come out there because people are already arriving with food. Maybe you two can have coffee in the den."

I followed Jeannie into the kitchen. "I'm afraid I'm here under false pretenses. I didn't know," I told her.

"Don't tell her. Let her think what she wants. She's so much more at peace since we found the note." Jeannie poured two cups of coffee and set them on a tray next to a plate of cinnamon buns. "Help yourself to cream and sugar. Mother takes hers black."

"The note? I don't understand." Apparently, the blow to the head had affected me more than I realized.

"The suicide note."

"Deke left a note?" I was impossibly slow on the uptake this morning.

Jeannie kept her patience with me. "Yes, in the dining room. Under a candlestick on the sideboard. That's where they left notes for one another, I guess, but I didn't know that. I'd brought a couple of boxes up there with me so I could get Mother's financial papers. When I saw the note, I just picked it up without looking at it. Yesterday, when I finally got around to go through everything, I realized what it was."

"Wait a minute. I don't understand. Deke said something in a note that made her feel better?"

"Don't ask me why, but somehow the note has given her closure. You can see the change in her, can't you?"

I had to admit I could. But Jeannie was lying. When I'd gone through the dining room on my way to check the front door, I'd walked over to that sideboard. I'd looked at it closely. There was no note there then. Maybe she was confused--certainly with all that had happened it would be understandable--but Jeannie didn't strike me as the type to get confused over something so simple.

As I carried the tray into the den, I puzzled over these new developments. Deke was dead; Ramona had accepted his death; Jeannie was lying about a suicide note.

Ramona chattered on about the funeral as she sipped her coffee. "I'm not sure when we can have it. They want to do an autopsy. I'll wear my good black dress. I have shoes to go with it."

I made appropriate responses to her ramblings and scrapped the questions I'd planned to ask. Obviously, this was not the time for them.

Ramona finished her coffee and set the cup back on the tray.

"Jeannie found the note Deke left. Did she tell you?" she said suddenly.

"Yes. Where did she find it?" I had to ask.

"Under a candlestick on the sideboard. That was our special place where we left notes for each other. He'd left it there before he went out to the cabin."

The same story. They were both mistaken about where the note was found. Unless...I didn't want to go this route, but I couldn't help myself. Could Jeannie have faked the note, thinking it would give her mother closure, as she called it, or for some other more ominous reason? Ramona was certainly calmer now, almost relieved, no longer talking about hearing someone in the cabin with Deke.

"Did he say why he did it?" I asked her.

"Money worries. Doesn't it always come down to money worries with men?"

"Does it? I guess I haven't thought about that."

"All you have to do is look around, Loren. You've got to see it." She stood up suddenly and went to the window. "Somebody's coming."

Ramona slid back the drape and peered out the window toward the back door. "Tom Bailey's out there. He's got his nerve. Looks like he's bringing a ham from Martinson's. One of those expensive ones too, I bet. Deke was so mad at him. He wouldn't dare come near us if Deke was still alive." She swiped at the tears which welled up each time she said Deke's name.

"Mad at Tom?" I could ask that much, couldn't I?

"Some business deal gone bad. Deke wouldn't tell me about it. Tom looks out for Number One. That's all Deke would say about him, but I've never seen him so upset. Now the minute Deke's gone, he trots over here with a ham, buttering up to Jeannie."

"To Jeannie? Why would he do that?"

"Oh, Jeannie's got her finger in so many pies around here. She's probably helping him sell his motel."

"Sell? I heard he was having a great year." Hadn't that been the gossip circulating all spring?

"Nothing's enough for some of these men. They always want more."

I was in too deep now to quit. Besides, we weren't really talking about Deke, were we?

"You think Tom is selling his motel? Why? Is he planning to do something else?" I asked.

"I don't know if he plans to sell it or is just taking a new mortgage on it. He went to the bank with Deke to see if we could borrow on our place, too. The bank wouldn't let us refinance. We owe too much already."

"Ramona, you've been going through a bad time. I'm so sorry."

"Poor Deke. It was all too much for him. That Tom Bailey was no help, leading him on with his big ideas."

"Big ideas?" What did that mean, I wondered. Wasn't this Mr. Roberts' problem, too?

"You know Tom. Wild schemes. Ways to make a fortune. He better not come in here, I tell you."

So, Tom was involved with Deke in some way. And with Jack and his father as well, judging from what had happened in the Taggerts' kitchen. I wondered what Ramona knew about that. Maybe if I gave her a chance to tell me...

"Tom had quite an argument with Jack at Taggerts' house last week. They almost came to blows," I said.

"I wish Jack had thrown a punch at him. He's such a wheeler-dealer. He deserves to have somebody stand up to him." Ramona sniffled again. This time the tears kept coming.

I'd said too much. I shouldn't have upset her. I found something else to talk about for a few minutes, then picked up the tray with our empty cups and carried it to the kitchen. Tom Bailey, the charming Tom this time, hovered close to Jeannie, murmuring in low tones. Whatever he was saying, she was lapping it up. I even thought I heard a girlish giggle as I walked in. I'd never realized Tom had such a way with the ladies. First, Melissa. Now, Jeannie. Could he be involved with either or both or them, or was I imagining things?

When Tom saw me, he broke off in mid-sentence and lost the charm. "Well, Mayor, sorry you had to see that blow-up at the Taggerts the other day. Did anyone tell you what we were arguing about?"

"Tom, my job gets me into enough arguments. I don't need to get involved in yours and Jack's." I reached for the doorknob.

I couldn't tell if he was relieved or annoyed by my answer, but he gave me a phony smile as I went out. Ramona was right--this guy sure didn't lack for nerve.

Chapter Thirty-four

I DROVE AWAY from Jeannie's house with even more unanswered questions than I'd arrived with. Deke had left a suicide note, but not in the place Jeannie claimed to have found it. The note had helped Ramona deal with her husband's death. Had she really believed the first story she told–that someone had argued with Deke in the cabin and murdered him? I couldn't begin to guess.

Tammy Stevenson had written five names in her little book. I'd failed to decode one. I'd put Jack on hold, since he'd refused to talk to me. Deke's death had forestalled my questions about him. That left me with two names: Peter Finch and Arthur Brown. I couldn't picture myself dropping by their homes to ask if they'd had an affair with a sixteen-year-old girl and paid her to keep silent about it. The sheriff's department might be making those very inquiries before too long, but they had the clout to get away with it. All I needed to destroy my relationship with Jim and the others in the sheriff's department was to leak sensitive information from Tammy's notebook before he made his move.

I'd driven half way home when I had an idea. Didn't I complain that Emerald Point natives like Kate and Pauline often knew the inside story on events, both past and present, I wasn't privy to? Sunday was Kate's day off. That made it a good time for questions and answers.

I found Kate in her kitchen, surrounded by simmering pots and tantalizing smells. She lifted a tray of fluffy biscuits out of the oven and insisted I try one.

I waved them away. "I'm full. I had breakfast with Ramona at Jeannie's. Did you know Deke died last night?"

"Yes, and I hear they found a suicide note. How's Ramona handling that? I'm sending over chicken and biscuits. It's a favorite of hers." She took a small plate from the cupboard, popped a biscuit onto it and set it in front of me.

As always, the news had traveled fast in Emerald Point. Here was Kate in her kitchen, up-to-date on the latest happening and engaged in her signature activity, making someone a gift of food.

The biscuit smelled heavenly. My resolve crumbled along with it as I popped a piece into my mouth and accepted the cup of coffee she poured to go with it

"Ramona seems to be taking things better than she was a couple of days ago," I said.

Kate sat down across from me at the table. "Glad to hear that."

"I bet you've also heard they found a notebook of Tammy Stevenson's with names in code." Why beat around the bush when Kate probably knew the whole story anyway?

"Josie's all excited. Seems she knows the code Tammy used, says she could have decoded it for Jim in a flash. Names of motel owners, I guess. You probably heard." She studied my face, waiting to see how much I knew about Tammy's list.

I nodded. "I heard Jack Roberts' name was one of them, but he's not about to discuss it with me. Deke Dolley and Peter Finch too. Has Jane said anything to you?"

Kate nodded sympathetically. She understood I was feeling my way along, gathering information. She shifted in her chair. She and Jane Finch were friends and she knew something. I didn't say anything more, just went on nibbling my biscuit as Kate weighed whether or not to share a confidence.

"This is between the two of us and I probably shouldn't tell you even," she said finally. "Peter had a thing with Tammy and Jane found out about it. A one-nighter, she called it. At least he swore it only happened once when he was drunk. As soon as he sobered up and realized how old she was, he was scared to death. Now he's terrified it will all come out. He could be looking at a statutory rape charge."

Was she assuming the others had made a similar mistake? I hardly knew what to ask first. "Did she say if Tammy asked him for money? Did he give her any?"

"Yeah, I guess that's how Jane found out. She was going through their checkbook and discovered a big chunk of money missing. Peter had suddenly stopped drinking and was moping around like the business was going under any minute. She pressed him and he finally told her what had happened."

"And she forgave him?" I never ceased to be amazed at how differently women reacted to that kind of news.

"Not exactly, but he begged her to stand by him at least for the time being. There's a lot at stake. They could even lose the motel."

"Why? Did he give her that much money?"

"Oh, Loren, I don't know, but it's an awful mess. I think Jane would talk to you if she thought you could help her keep this thing quiet."

"Keep something like this quiet in Emerald Point? I'd have to be a miracle worker. The story's already out there. In a day or two, everybody going to know about that notebook."

Kate slid another biscuit onto my plate. "I suppose. But Jane's clutching at straws right now."

"I would like to hear what she has to say, but I can't very well go knock on her door and ask her," I said.

Before I realized what she was doing, Kate had picked up the phone and was tapping out a number.

"Jane, Loren Graham's here. She's trying to unravel that code Tammy Stevenson left." Silence. Kate listened, her face devoid of expression. "She'd be very discreet. I don't see what you've got to lose. Somebody from the sheriff's office will be around looking for answers soon enough."

Kate turned from the phone to ask me. "Would you meet her at Randy Smith's for coffee in twenty minutes?"

I nodded, grateful to Kate for intervening. "Thanks for your help. Maybe I'll find answers for some of my own questions if I talk with her."

JANE FINCH WAS already seated in a back booth waiting for me when I arrived at the coffee shop a short time later. Tall and slim, her long brown hair held back in a scrunchie, Jane, under ordinary circumstances, could have passed for a young woman in her twenties. Today, dark circles under her eyes and deep crevices on both sides of her mouth made her look older than her forty-five years.

"Thank you for meeting me," she said.

I ordered a ginger ale--one more drop of caffeine would have pushed me over the edge–and let her take the initiative.

She got right to it.

"You've heard about the notebook. It just a matter of time before the sheriff's office figures out those names and numbers and what they mean."

"Has Peter thought about talking to someone first, before anyone comes to him?"

"And saying what? That he had sex with an underage girl? That would be a criminal offense, wouldn't it?" Jane ducked her head, hiding her face. She kept her voice so low I could hardly make out her words.

"No, I'm not suggesting that. He should be very careful what he admits to. Peter needs to hire an attorney, the best one you can find."

"Loren, we can't afford an attorney. We're broke. If Peter's charged with anything, he might have to ask for a public defender."

I stared at her, not sure what this meant. "Wait. Are you saying he gave Tammy that much money, enough so you can't put your hands on any more?"

"He swears he only gave her five hundred dollars. He paid it in two installments, three hundred one time and two hundred another. He says that's what she got from the others, too. But our books seem to be in really bad shape. When we bought the motel, we thought we'd made a good decision. Jeannie Spenser brokered the deal for us, got us a good price for our motel in Lake George and talked the people we bought from here into coming down."

"But it was still too much to handle. Is that the problem?"

Jane shook her head. "I don't know. There's some business deal Peter doesn't want to tell me about. He insisted I stop asking him, says it's better that I don't know."

"I suppose he's trying to protect you. But it's too late for that now. Jane, you have to hire a good lawyer, even if you feel you can't afford it. You need advice."

"Is that what Jack is going to do?"

I looked at her blankly for a minute before the light dawned. She thought I already knew what Jack planned to do. That was the reason she'd agreed to talk with me.

"He's got his problems, too, I understand," she went on. "Sounds like that girl was blackmailing old Jack the same way she was Peter. He's mucked up good this time, I guess, maybe even more than young Jack can fix."

I gaped at her, as stupefied as if she'd spoken in a language I'd never heard before. "Are you saying old Jack? You mean John, Jack's father?"

"I've always heard him called Jack. A lot of people who've lived around the lake for a long time still call him Jack."

I answered automatically, my thoughts a blur. "They do? I guess I never paid much attention."

"He made the switch to John some years ago after young Jack came back to town. Hated being called old Jack. I can't say as I blame him. I used to be called little Jane in my hometown, even after I'd grown to be 5'9"."

"Your mother was Jane, too, I take it." I struggled to assimilate this new idea. When Tammy listed the name in her notebook, was she referring to Mr. Roberts, rather than Jack?

"A pretty stupid move on the old man's part getting involved with a young girl like that. Some folks think he's lost it big time. Others say young Jack's made too many changes, made his father feel obsolete," she said.

I couldn't come up with a comment. Was the Jack Roberts in the notebook Jack's father? It was possible, wasn't it? Tammy's parents had lived here all their lives. They probably spoke of the older man as Jack, and Tammy would be apt to think of him that way too. Jane could be right.

"Peter's made a lot of changes in his life in the last year," she went on. "He's stopped drinking–he would never have gotten involved with a young girl like that if he hadn't been drunk, you know. And he treats me much better. He's scared to death, Loren. It's like something finally knocked some sense into him."

"So things between you are better than they were?" I said.

"Well, for now anyway. We decided we'd take this one day at a time. Unless, of course, he ends up going to jail."

"Do you think that could happen?"

"It could, I suppose. I'm not sure I can live with this for the long term, but I've agreed to stick by him for now. That's all I've promised him."

Jane knew about her husband's mistake and was hanging in there. Jack Roberts and I had been friends for a long time. At least I'd thought we were friends. Whatever he'd done or hadn't done, why couldn't he have told me about it and expected me to understand instead of slamming a door in my face.

CHApter THirty-five

MONDAY MORNING I opened the door to my office a few minutes after seven. The night had dragged endlessly. Torments I'd escaped Saturday night by falling into an exhausted sleep had regrouped their forces and pummeled me with a vengeance. I relived the attack at the campsite, the break-in at the house. For hours I stared wide-eyed into the misty light outside my windows, as jumpy as one of Rogers' Rangers expecting a French attack at dawn.

To make matters worse, my mind insisted on sorting through the strange bits and pieces of information I'd picked up in the past few days. I was seeing connections I didn't understand. Four local hotel or motel owners were suffering financial problems. Both Peter Finch and Jack's father had been hit with losses they couldn't or wouldn't account for. Deke Dolley had killed himself rather than face his money worries. Phil Johnson's complaints coincided with rumors that the Beach House, too, was struggling to survive.

These businesses formed the bedrock of our local economy. The tourists who stayed at them frequented our restaurants, shopped in our stores, brought money into our community in ways too numerous to count. These hotels and motels provided the jobs local families counted on. The loss of even one of them would be a serious blow to the town. The loss of all of them could turn us into a ghost town.

Tammy Stevenson provided a common thread. If her notebook could be believed, she'd gotten money from three of these owners. Phil Johnson wasn't listed in the notebook, at least not in the names I'd deciphered, but I wouldn't rule him out.

Still, according to Jane Finch, the amounts Tammy received were piddling, two to five hundred dollars, not enough to break anyone. It was hard to believe a blackmail scheme which involved so little money could undermine so many businesses. There had to be something more.

Tammy had listed another local motel owner--Arthur Brown--and entered and crossed out only one figure after his name–200. I didn't know much about Arthur's business, but I had an idea how I could find out.

BEFORE THE LAST center meeting Arthur had presented me with a diorama of the lake bottom his grandson had fashioned out of plaster and mounted on a large piece of plywood. I'd already spoken to Stephanie about writing an article on the diorama as part of our ongoing efforts to publicize the center. This would provide a good excuse to talk to Arthur.

I unlocked the door to the small storage room next to my office where the diorama was stored. Here was a part of our world most of us never saw–the underwater peaks and valleys, the trenches and plains carved by glaciers as they retreated millions of years ago. The boy had even included small replicas–the bateaux, the radeau, broken sections of docks, even cannon balls from long ago battles. He'd researched everything, positioning the artifacts just where divers had found them. The map was a masterpiece of accuracy, and yet I remembered Matt Tremont's words. Things moved around down there, he'd said; nobody could ever be sure, really sure, where they might end up.

When Pauline arrived a little after noon, I waited until she had her desk arranged to her liking, my time-tested practice. Then I pounced. "Pauline, the names in Tammy Stevenson's notebook–what's the latest you've heard?"

Pauline could have pretended ignorance, but that wasn't her style. If she chose to speak about something, she spoke the truth. The door to the storeroom stood open. She glanced toward the diorama.

"Too bad when people start gossiping like that. Heard Arthur Brown was one of 'em and I know that's a crock. If Arthur gave her money, he gave it as a gift, not to cover up anything he did. I'd stake my life on that."

"You think so?" I said. Money given as a gift, not to buy silence. It was possible, I supposed.

"I know so. If she told Arthur she was pregnant, like folks say she was doing, he'd help her just because that's the way he is. Anyway, he's older than Reggie and his health's been failing. I doubt he could manage much of any philandering even if he wanted to, which I'm sure he didn't."

I considered her words. Pauline was loyal to a fault–to Reggie, to Young Ned, to old friends like Arthur Brown. But, how did this thinking jibe with Kate's talk about the Blue Angel and other May-December liaisons?

Still, Pauline wasn't granting absolution across the board.

"I'm not saying age alone rules out that kind of hanky panky. There's no fool like an old fool, you know. Now Jack Roberts, he's always been kind of a ladies' man, maybe thinks he still is."

"John, you mean?" I said.

"Why yes, people are saying she meant the father. Now that you mention it...well, I guess I don't know for sure about that. Maybe she was talking about young Jack."

Nothing definite there.

"What about the others? What do you think about them?"

"Deke Dolley upped and shot himself. Could be 'cause his name's in the notebook, could be he had some other reason. I expect Ramona will deny he was involved with the girl. That's what Jane Finch is doing, I hear. Now Phil Johnson–his wife's out of the picture. He's got nobody to defend him."

That did it. I had the fifth name. Another hotel owner, and another business with financial problems. Maybe I hadn't taken Phil's string of complaints seriously enough.

"Phil's been doing a lot of complaining about his business," I said.

Pauline nodded in agreement. "That's Phil for you. His grandfather owned the entire Point, you know. Valuable piece of property with a lumber yard and sawmill on it. The father ran up big debts and sold off the northern half of it to recoup his losses."

"That must have been years ago."

"Sure, and Phil's been crying poor mouth ever since. But he never got his act together to buy it back. Wife got sick of hearing it. Part of the reason she left him, folks said. He ought to find a way to get the Beach House out of the red or give it up."

So Phil Johnson was the fifth name, the one I'd failed to decipher. That put all five men listed in Tammy's book in what Jack liked to call the hospitality industry–Phil Johnson, Deke, Jack or his father, Peter Finch and Arthur Brown. Pauline had nothing but praise for Arthur Brown and the amount after his name didn't jibe with the others. Maybe I could start by crossing him off the list.

An hour later I parked in front of Brown's Colonial Motel. One the most appealing motels in the area, the Colonial consisted of two rows of attached rooms, painted a soft yellow and surrounded by attractively landscaped grounds. If Arthur and I exhausted the topic of the diorama and the prospects for the summer season, I'd have to improvise.

Arthur admitted me to his office with a smile and a handshake. He was past seventy now, shrunken and stooped, but with a thick head of white hair and black button eyes which gave him a merry look.

I opened the conversation with my prepared remarks.

"I think I can get the *Post Standard* to do a series of features on the center and I'd like to kick off with a piece on your grandson's diorama–if you think that would be all right with him."

"He'd be flattered, I'm sure, but you'll want to talk to him about it." Arthur tore a sheet of paper off a pad and wrote down his grandson's name and phone number.

"I plan to call him. But since you brought it in, I wanted to make sure you didn't have any problems with our publicizing it."

"The boy will be pleased you want to use it. You won't have any trouble getting him to agree–and to help out in any way he can. You do, just give me a call."

"I appreciate this, Arthur. He did a great job. I can see using it as a permanent display, if we ever get the center up and running."

"You will, Loren. Don't worry. You're moving heaven and earth for this town–most folks know that--not sneaking around like some who only want to line their own pockets."

What did that mean? I framed a cautious reply. "There are those who do, I grant you that."

"Call themselves a consortium–whatever that means–a fancy name for a bunch of schemers if you ask me. You're headed in the right direction, young lady. Don't let anybody tell you different."

A consortium. Could I get him to tell me what he meant?

"Arthur, sometimes it's hard being an outsider in a tight-knit community. You hear disturbing things and you wonder what to think about them."

Arthur chuckled. If he knew I was fishing, he was decent enough not make me keep at it.

"Most recently about a dead gal's notebook, I suspect. Heard I'm in it along with the young studs. In a way, it's kind of flattering for an old geezer like me gettin' that sort of mention."

"Is it really?" I asked with a smile.

"There's another side to it, not so nice. My grandson asked me about it a couple days ago. I could see he was having trouble thinking of me linked to a girl a few years older than him."

"How did you deal with that?"

"Told him the truth, that's all, and he seemed to believe me. He knows I've helped kids, given them money for college applications and the like. A few years ago I got up a group of alumni from colleges around here to take kids to look at places they were interested in. Some parents don't give 'em any encouragement along those lines at all, you know. It's a shame."

"So you've done that yourself?"

"Did it myself for a long time. Not so much any more. I'm getting too old for traipsing around those big campuses, but there's those willing to do it. People taking their own kid to look at a college don't mind bringing a couple extras along, especially when I slip 'em a little money toward the trip. The guidance counselors keep me posted, give me names of deserving youngsters in need of money for applications. Poor family can have trouble even with those first steps, you know."

I was off on another track. "Tammy Stevenson, Arthur? Was anyone trying to help her?"

"There's those that tried. I gave a couple of hundred dollars for her applications, but she didn't much want to be helped. Smart enough, that girl, but used her smarts wrong. Sad. Turned out bad for her, bad for her family, bad for the town."

I agreed. Arthur had summed it up well. He'd sounded convincing, and he'd explained the 200 after his name in the notebook to my satisfaction. But I wanted to get back to his earlier statement.

"You mentioned a consortium, Arthur. I guess I don't know much about that."

"Sounds high class, doesn't it? But don't be fooled. A bunch of 'em invited me in. I turned 'em down fast. I told John Roberts not to be fooled, either. I never did like the way Tom Bailey did business. Speculative land deals aren't my cup of tea."

"Speculative? Something here in town, you mean?" I knew better than to push like that, but I couldn't stop myself.

Arthur pursed his lips. "Not at liberty to say right now. You go ahead and call the boy. I suspect he'll tell you to use that diorama any way you see fit. He'll be tickled to death and so will I." He reached across the desk and extended his hand. I got the message. I stood up and we shook hands.

Great. I'd finally learned something and I had no idea what it was. A consortium. Speculative land deals. Was a group of our hotel and motel owners engineering those so-called better things Jeannie Spenser had referred to? And why wasn't anyone willing to talk about them?

CHAPTER THIRTY-SIX

A HALF HOUR later I was seated at the bar of the Beach House on the Point, sipping a glass of Chardonnay–okay, so it was a little early in the day--and chatting up Phil Johnson as he rearranged bottles behind the bar. I was his only customer. Out on the terrace a waitress was clearing and resetting two empty tables. The lunch business– whatever there'd been of it–was over.

I'd prepared for this chat too. I started with an easy question.

"Phil, did you think any more about talking to the Council about the trailer park and the campground or have things improved over there?"

Phil took his time deciding on an answer. He poured himself a generous slug of Scotch and came around the bar to sit on a stool next to me. "Can't say there's been any improvement. Quiet one night, then all hell breaks loose the next."

I rephrased the question. "Did you think any more about making a complaint?"

"I don't know, Loren. Tell you the truth I'd like to be shut of this whole business."

I gave him a disbelieving look. "You'd never give up the Beach House, Phil. It's been in your family–what?–three generations, anyway."

Phil drained off the Scotch remaining in his glass and stood up. Another conversation over, I thought. But no. He ambled around the bar and poured himself an even heftier drink.

He sat back down next to me. "Not worth ending up like Deke Dolley with my brains splashed all over a wall."

"Things aren't that bad, are they? Why, Jeannie Spenser is full of confidence about the future, hinting at better times ahead."

"Yeah, that chance to grab the brass ring she likes to talk about."

I loved rolling out bad clichés in a good cause. "That too. And better things on the horizon–let's not forget that. But what the hell does it all mean, Phil? Your neighbors aren't selling out, are they? Been some strange rumors around town."

Phil's eyebrows shot up. Suddenly, he was the one asking the questions. "What kind of rumors?"

I hadn't lied–well, not exactly. Strange rumors circulated almost daily at the Point.

"Some kind of consortium, Phil. You probably know more than I do, since you're in the hospitality business."

"What the hell you talking about, Loren?"

"I'm telling you there's been a lot of gossip. And I expect you know why. Almost more talk than about Tammy Stevenson's notebook."

His cheek twitched. His worried expression coupled with his remark about Deke encouraged me to keep digging. "There's a rumor a group's making plans for the Point right now. Maybe you know about that, Phil."

I'd taken a stab in the dark, but I could tell from his expression it had hit its mark. "You should know better than to believe everything you hear in this town, Loren."

"On the other hand, secrets don't stay secrets very long, either. Some pretty convincing stuff making the rounds out there. Like that consortium I mentioned."

Phil dropped his head in his hands. I'd hit pay dirt.

"It's a mess, Loren. I should never have gotten involved. Started out simple enough. A group of us did get together, formed that consortium you're talking about."

I knew that much. I wanted details.

"To do what, Phil?"

"We chipped in money, planned to buy the rest of the Point. We heard about somebody wanting to build here, but they needed it all. I owned this here part with the Beach House, except they weren't going to use the building. They were going to tear it down and build new after we got rid of the campground."

Finally, I saw it–it had been right under my nose.

"You mean you've been trying to force the campground owners out, Phil? That's why you were complaining so much?"

"Those people didn't take much interest in the place anyway. Looked like if we gave 'em a few problems they'd sell fast enough."

"So you made the trouble over there yourself?"

"I helped it along. Didn't take much doing. Some of my kitchen help riled things up a little."

"You did this for what, Phil? To build another hotel, to land some big franchise?" I said in disgust.

"Jeez, Loren. Give me a break. Not a hotel. A casino. Gambling–that would mean money for everybody."

I heard the words, but I couldn't grasp their meaning.

"What are you saying, Phil? You can't just go ahead and build a gambling casino. There are laws against it."

"Don't be too sure. You might be wrong about that."

"You're as far off base as George Tyler. Indians–Native Americans, that is–they're the only ones can have casinos in New York State," I insisted.

"Right now, maybe."

"And they can only have them on the reservations. These aren't Indian lands around here."

"Loren, haven't you heard the State's going to relax restrictions on gambling? When they do, the Point will be the perfect spot for it. Far enough from Atlantic City to draw from downstate, western New York, New England. We'd even get the Canadians back if the exchange rate ever improves for 'em."

"But, Phil, casinos have to be built on tribal lands. Even George Tyler knows that."

"George isn't keeping up with what's happening. The State's thinking about allowing something new: off-reservation gambling, they call it. A tribe will be able to acquire property right here on the Point, and it can become sovereign land. Land Into Trust is the official name."

"Here? On Emerald Point?" I still didn't believe what he was telling me.

"Right here. Then we can join forces with them and go ahead and build a casino. Do you have any idea what that would mean, Loren? We'd be looking at millions, millions! Emerald Point could be the biggest guy on the block, big as Foxwoods!"

I struggled to understand. The first time I'd seen Foxwoods, I'd thought my eyes were playing tricks on me. It rose out of the Connecticut woods like a colossus, like a palace from a fairy tale, blue-green turrets glistening in the sunlight, entry roads and parking lots clogged with cars and buses.

"Think about it, Loren. You wouldn't be worrying about our economy, then. We'd have tourists streaming in, hundreds of jobs, new hotels and restaurants--everything we ever wanted. Even a loudmouth like George Tyler could see that."

"But George brought this subject up at a meeting and people turned on him. You were there."

"Not the right time for it. And George wasn't the right guy to do it."

"You're talking about casino gambling, here at Emerald Point? Is that what this has all been about, Phil?"

I tried again to make sense of his words. I could see why the idea was tempting, but the problems that would come with it were mind boggling. I thought more like a mayor now than a private citizen. What about Northway exits and access roads, trash and sewage disposal, the air and water pollution we'd have to deal with? And those were just the immediate concerns. We'd be a prime target for outside interests trying to take us over and for the evils legalized gambling would bring. And what about the lake? That had to be our first, our foremost consideration. The lake was our most valuable asset. What would rapid, uncontrolled growth do to our lake?

"Gambling, Phil. You don't really want that here, do you?"

"Look, Loren, it's a fact of life. It's going to happen. We can be making the money instead of people somewhere else. The Catskills are nearly dead now because of the Atlantic city gambling. You don't think that can happen to us, too, if we don't move on this? I'm tellin' you in three or four years our consortium could be bringing in a billion dollars a year."

"Who's in this consortium? Arthur Brown told me he turned thumbs down on the idea. Who's in this with you?"

He glanced around the bar. The waitress had finished clearing the terrace and disappeared into the kitchen. Even so, he lowered his voice to a whisper. "Deke was, until he chickened out."

"Are you saying Deke killed himself over this?"

"God, Loren, I don't know. We all put in money for lobbying. A guy named Webb handled that for us. Deke chipped in what he could get his hands on, but he couldn't borrow any more. He was going to lose what he'd put in. He wanted this bad. Ramona was always the brains, you know? He thought he could show her that he could do something smart."

"And look how he ended up. This is a wild scheme, Phil. Are you sure you know what you're doing?"

"Walk over there with me right now, let me show you what we'd have if it all went through. Put our town on the map. You should be happy about that."

Nothing he'd said so far had made me happy, but I walked out with him to see what he wanted to show me.

As we crossed the Beach House lawn, I noticed that the temperature had tumbled in the short time I'd been inside. The wind came barreling off the lake; thunderheads gathered over the mountains. I shivered in my light jacket.

"So, you're saying for this scheme to work, your consortium needs to own all of the Point," I said as we approached the trailer park.

"My land and the park together would give us just enough. Now tell me it would be a great loss if this place shut down. Take a close look," Phil said.

I understood what he meant. In the daylight, I was getting a better sense of why Phil had found fault. This wasn't the lively, brightly colored campground I'd thought I was seeing that night from the Beach House lawn. The colored lights, turned off in the daytime, drooped from the wires overhead. The shells of the trailers were chipped; the awnings, faded and tattered. No sign of the vacationers staying here. They probably spent their afternoons at the beach.

"Look at the mess that's been made here." Phil swept his hand around in an expansive gesture that almost knocked him off balance.

As we reached the section reserved for tents, I spotted the dirt road leading to Todd Lewis's site. Sharp gusts of wind, stronger and colder now, sent dirt and leaves scurrying along the ground. I pulled my jacket tightly around me.

"We're going to get a bad storm, Phil. Let's start walking back."

"Just a little further, Loren. I want to show you where we'd build."

"I got jumped here the other night, you know," I reminded him.

"Heard about it. Don't worry. If that guy comes back, I'll be right here to protect you." Phil tried for a Clint Eastwood-like swagger.

I wasn't reassured. If I needed a protector, I'd want someone a lot steadier on his feet than Phil Johnson.

Chapter Thirty-seven

As we rounded a bend in the dirt road, two men emerged from the trees. Tom Bailey and the man I'd seen surveying with him the night I was attacked sauntered along, obviously checking out the area. Were they members of Phil's consortium, too? Somehow Tom managed to keep popping up.

"Tom, what's happening?" Phil shouted. His greeting sounded forced, ingratiating.

Tom stepped up the pace as he approached us.

"What the hell you doing over here, Phil?"

"Showing the Mayor around a little. She's trying to get me to file a complaint about these campgrounds."

"You seem to spend a lot of time here yourself, Tom. I saw you here a few nights ago, didn't I?" I said.

The man with Tom Bailey double-timed up to us. He wore a business suit and wing tipped Cordovans, a strange outfit for a walk in a dusty campground. My memory cells scurried around trying to place the shoes. I'd seen them some place before. But where?

"Why the hell you want him to file a complaint, Mayor?" Tom shot an exasperated look at Phil.

"Just part of my official duties to suggest it, Tom. Phil's been complaining about this part of the Point. I wanted to see what he was talking about."

"Told you I had clout with the Mayor." Phil favored me with a sheepish grin. His slurred speech testified to his recent Scotches.

Tom's face twisted into a fierce scowl, the same face I'd seen in Taggerts' kitchen when he argued with Jack.

"Damn it, Phil. You're drunk. And what time is it–not three in the afternoon? That's great, just great."

I didn't stop to edit what I was saying. The minute I recognized the man with Tom, I turned to him.

"Wait. I know who you are. You're the guy stumbled on the snake in the bathroom at Tom's motel," I said.

Tom swung around to face me, glaring, his hands clenching into fists at his side. "What the hell you talking about, Mayor?"

"The rattlesnake in the bathroom, Tom. You remember. The deputies were called to your motel to capture it. I'd gone down there looking for Jim Thompson. This is the man who rented the room from you." As if Tom didn't know that.

Not satisfied by what they'd already accomplished, my busy little memory cells sent another recollection up the pipe. I turned back to his companion. "Then I saw you at the bar at the Emerald Point Inn talking with Mr. Roberts. I'm Loren Graham. I didn't get your name."

The man swiveled from me to Tom and back, a confused expression clouding his face. "Brian Webb. Pleased to meet you," he muttered finally. He didn't sound the least bit pleased.

Tom puffed up, ready to explode. What was it with Tom? He could sure drop that genial manner in a hurry.

Brian Webb's eyes narrowed.

Suddenly, the picture took shape, became clearer. These men were part of the consortium Arthur Brown and Phil had been talking about.

"I never heard if they found that rattler did you, Mr. Webb? I suppose it's one of the things that come crawling in here sometimes, if we're not on our toes. They can slither in before we know what's going on, but we don't encourage them to hang around." I spun around fast and walked away.

Phil caught up with me as I hurried along the dirt road leading out of the campground. "Damn it, Loren, what the hell were you doing back there? You shouldn't have said those things."

Maybe he was right. I'd blurted out my remarks without thinking, but something else was nagging at me now, something that stayed just beyond my memory's range. I kept reaching for it, but it slipped away each time I came close. Talking about the rattlesnake incident had reminded me of something. A remark in passing, something about Tom and his motel. I'd been talking to someone, talking about an entirely different matter. There'd been a comment made, a comment which had barely registered at the time. I was talking on the phone–I had it finally–to Jim Thompson a few days after Brian Webb had found the rattlesnake in the bathroom of Tom's motel.

"You could have asked Tom Bailey about Tammy Stevenson," Jim had said, "if he wasn't so upset about that snake. She worked for him for a while."

That was what I was trying to remember. Tom Bailey was linked to Tammy Stevenson, too. Another motel owner and--if my guess was right--a member of the consortium. But he wasn't listed in Tammy's book. He was a friend of Bob Taggert's, a friend of Melissa's, too, maybe more than a friend of Mel's, as he called her. Why wasn't Tom Bailey on Tammy's list of people she'd worked for and asked for money?

As we entered the trailer park, I heard an ominous crack over my head, a loud, menacing pop like a gun going off. Blasts of wind whipped the branches above us into a frenzy of movement. Leaves shook their pale undersides. A shower of twigs cascaded down on us as we backtracked toward the Beach House.

I stopped suddenly. Phil pulled up beside me. I could see branches sway and dip over the road. One of the biggest limbs on an old pine trembled, knifed downward, then crashed to the ground a few feet ahead of us.

The people staying at the park stampeded up the hill from the lake, many of them struggling with coolers and beach paraphernalia. Families rushed by trying to get out from under the trees. Parents carried babies and pulled small children by their hands.

Phil shouted orders to the crowd. "You people, go to the Beach House. Tell whoever's at the desk Phil said to let you stay in the lobby. You're not safe here."

One of the smaller trailers, buffeted by the winds, slid off its concrete blocks and tilted sideways. As the crowd surged past, a woman raced toward us screaming. "Help me! Help me! My baby's in there!"

We watched in disbelief as the wind hit her and knocked her off her feet. I grabbed hold of her arm and pulled her upright.

"Show us where. We'll help you."

"My baby! I left him taking a nap. I just came outside for a minute." She was crying as we struggled to move forward.

The trailer toppled further to the side, scraping along the length of a big pine with an ear-splitting screech until it was wedged tight. The woman screamed again.

Bent over almost double, she and I stumbled toward the trailer. The door was jammed shut against the tree. She tugged on the handle in a desperate attempt to open it. Phil put his hands on both sides of hers and pulled. The door didn't budge.

"What about that window?" I said.

The back window of the trailer had been slid part way open. Only a small screen covered the space, but even with the trailer tipped to the side, the window was too far off the ground for us to reach it.

"Help me up. Maybe I can crawl in and get him," the woman said. Without waiting for me to respond, she jumped up and grabbed the thin metal ledge under the window and tried to pull herself up.

"Wait. Let me see if I can lift you." I cupped my hands and she stuck one foot into them. It took all my strength to raise her even a few inches higher. As she ripped at the screen, a blast of wind smashed into her, breaking her hold on the ledge and knocking her to the ground. She cried out and clutched her arm with the opposite hand. She rolled back and forth in pain on the ground, her cries snatched away by the wind.

"We gotta get some help over here." Phil yelled and took off toward the hotel.

The gale increased in velocity. Patio chairs and tables, many of them lightweight aluminum, tumbled along the ground, dangerous missiles crashing into anything in their path. One metal chair lay on its side on the patio, caught up against the trailer. I picked it up and wedged it under the window. As I tried to stand on it, the wind caught me and tossed me off as easily as if I'd been rag doll. I fell heavily, scraping my leg along a concrete block.

"I need your help. Can you use your good arm?" I asked the woman, still writhing on the ground.

She struggled to her feet, hugging her injured arm.

"Maybe if you braced your body against the chair I could climb up," I told her.

She grimaced with pain, but she leaned her weight against the chair. I climbed onto the seat and raised one foot until I could wedge it between the chair back and the wall. I lifted my body slowly until I got my other foot onto the chair back. The mother had already ripped the screen. I seized the edges and tore at them until the screen came loose. I could see inside. A little boy about two years old was seated on the floor, his face streaked with tears. He cuddled a worn blue blanket against his cheek and sucked his thumb as he cried silently. His eyes were wide with fright.

"He's scared, but otherwise he seems okay. What's his name?" I asked his mother.

I could hear the relief in her voice. "Jamie. His name is Jamie. Are you sure he's all right? Can you reach him?"

I took stock of the opening. The child would probably fit through it, but it was too small for an adult. I spoke slowly with more confidence than I felt. "Jamie, I'm Loren. I want to lift you out through the window. Can you walk over to me?"

The child sucked harder on his thumb.

"Your mommy's here. She wants me to pick you up for her."

An extra strong gust of wind started the chair tipping. As I clung to the window ledge, I shifted my head just enough to call down to the mother. "You've got to let him know you're here. Wait until there's a lull and call his name. Tell him to let me pick him up."

The mother shouted Jamie's name again and again. He brightened a little when he recognized her voice, but he continued to eye me with suspicion. It took repeated cajoling from both of us before he tottered along the uneven floor and came near enough for me to get a grip on him.

I took hold of his shoulders and pulled him closer. "Good boy, Jamie. I'm going to lift you up and swing you down to your mother."

"Tell me what to do," the mother said anxiously. "I can only use one arm. I can't hang onto the chair and take him from you too."

"Try to keep the chair steady as long as you can. Then let go and grab him."

I pulled my upper body out of the window slowly, my arms straining with the child's weight. Jamie was a chunky little guy. I moved cautiously, tugging him through the opening, trying not to scrape his bare legs against the jagged remnants of the screen. As I started to hand him down to his mother, he caught sight of her standing below us. He squirmed in my arms, shoving against me. The wind smashed into us; the chair tipped, righted itself, tipped again. I lowered Jamie toward his mother and grabbed for the ledge. My fingers slipped along the smooth metal. I pushed out from the trailer wall, twisting my body to avoid landing on Jamie as the three of us crashed to the ground. I felt a sharp blow as my head struck one of the concrete blocks supporting the trailer. Darkness swept over me, blocking out everything else.

178

CHAPTER THIRTY-EIGHT

I CAME AWAKE slowly. I lay crumpled on the ground. My head throbbed with pain. Flashes of light zigzagged behind my eyes like bolts of lightning. My limbs felt paralyzed with cold; my clothes were soaked from the rain. I couldn't seem to move.

Over the sound of Jamie's wails, I heard the woman calling to me, repeating the same words over and over like a mantra.

"Sit up. Try to sit up."

I couldn't sit up. I couldn't even answer her.

She set Jamie, still crying, on the grass and slid her good arm under my head.

"Sit up slow. Be careful."

I tried to do as she said, but my head lay like dead weight against her arm. The trailer, the trees, everything around me spun in an insane dance. The black skies pressed down like leaden weights, scorching my face with rain and wind.

I heard another voice. "Here, I'll help her. Take the little boy and run to the Beach House. You've got to get him out of here."

"I can't leave her here. She got my baby out for me," the woman said.

"I'll take care of her. Don't worry about it. Just go."

The spinning slowed a little. I eased myself up on one elbow. I didn't see anyone, but I got a sense of movement behind me. Before I could turn around, something struck me on the back of the head. I reeled and fell sideways into darkness. I had no idea how long I'd been lying there when I forced my eyes open once again and tried to lift my head.

"Hit her. She's still alive. It'll look like an accident," another voice said.

The voice sounded familiar, but muffled, indistinct. Or, was the ringing in my head distorting the sound of it?

I heard running footsteps coming toward me.

"What the hell's going on, you guys? Jesus. Is that the mayor? What happened to her?" Phil. I thought it was Phil Johnson's voice, but it was hard to be sure with the tumult in my head.

Another voice, garbled, unrecognizable. "You told her too much, you fool. With that and what she's figured out herself, she can blow the whistle on us. You want to see everything we worked for go down the tubes?"

"I never agreed to murder. I know her. She's the mayor, for God sake. That makes her death front page news." That was Phil. I was sure of it now.

"Women. First that little slut and her stupid notebook, and now this nosey bitch. She's a worse snoop than the kid was."

Another voice. "Damn it. You can't kill her, especially not here, not right where they'd want to build. We got too many problems with this damn site already."

"Let's get out of here then. Maybe she'll die on her own." The sound of their voices moved away, floating back to me from a distance.

I didn't know how long I lay there, chilled through, weak, so shaky I didn't think I could stand. The lights flashed on and off behind my eyes. They'd sent Jamie and his mother away from here. I had to get away, too.

I raised my body slowly, first to my knees, then to my feet. My clothes dripped water. My head throbbed with excruciating pain. I thought I was going to throw up. I ran a hand cautiously over the places where I hurt most, relieved not to feel any blood.

As soon as I could gather the strength, I tottered to a tree, hung on the trunk for a few minutes, then launched myself toward another one. The ground was littered with branches, limbs, even entire trees uprooted by the force of the storm.

I was alone now. Rain and dirt swirled around me. My eyes stung from the water and dust. I could scarcely see. When I came to a sturdy looking maple, I leaned against it, then slid down to sit with my head resting against the bark.

I forced myself to get up. I staggered on with no sense of the direction I was headed in. After every few steps, I stopped and tried to spot the Beach House roof through the trees. Even with the piles of branches on the ground, I couldn't find an open space in the churning canopy overhead.

A man emerged from the shadows. I cowered away from him, not knowing if he was one of the men who'd attacked me.

He moved closer. "If you're trying to get to the Beach House, you're headed the wrong way."

I turned slowly. Everywhere I looked the darkness bulged with shadowy forms, tree trunks, hanging limbs. I would have welcomed flashes of lightning, but the worst of the storm had passed.

I couldn't make out the man's face. His features were a blur. Was it one of the men who'd talked about killing me? I couldn't tell. My foot caught in a downed branch. I stumbled, pitched forward, staggered toward him. As I careened into him, I saw the shoes, the wing-tipped Cordovans. I raised my eyes to his face. It was Brian Webb, the man from Tom Bailey's motel, from the bar at the Inn, the man with Tom at the campgrounds. He'd realized I knew about the gambling scheme. Had he been the one who wanted to kill me?

I backed away from him. "Stay away from me. I know where I'm going."

"I don't think you do. I'll take you to the Beach House." He gripped my arm tight, too tight.

"Let go of me. I'll get myself there."

He didn't answer. He shoved me along, barely dodging the piles of fallen branches.

"Let me go." I was shouting now. I tried to pull away from him, but he hung on to my arm.

He whipped me around, flung me to the ground.

"What the..."

"Why didn't you die when that limb came down on you?" He stood over me, his face dark, malevolent, contorted by rage.

I'd fallen backward into a pile of branches. They cut like knives, but I pulled my legs under me and forced my hands down through the mess until they closed around a thick limb at the bottom of the pile.

Brian Webb raised his arm. The cords on his neck stood out. "Maybe you did die, maybe you just haven't gotten around to it yet."

I stared up at him, trying to comprehend his words.

He was holding something, brandishing it above his head–a branch, a club, I couldn't tell which. He was going to kill me. He was going to kill me, and I didn't know why.

Everything happened in slow motion. The limb shifted in the pile beneath me. I clung tight to it with both hands and yanked it free. I tensed, raised myself up as far as I could and swung the limb like a baseball bat just as Webb brought the club down toward my head. I caught him hard across the knees and rolled to the side. I heard the awful, hollow sound of the limb striking him, heard a bone crack, heard his scream of pain. His blow missed my head and glanced off my shoulder. I knew I'd been hit, but I didn't feel anything.

I scrambled out of the pile, crawling away from him until I reached a flat place where I could stand. A fresh burst of adrenaline gave me the strength to run. I glanced back just long enough to see him doubled over, hugging his left knee. I thought he couldn't step on his left foot, but I wasn't sure. I kept the branch with me and ran.

Not certain of my direction, I stumbled through the campground, too terrified to look back to see if Brian Webb was following me. Where were the others? Phil had stopped them from killing me once, but then Webb had come back to finish me off. And who was the third man standing over me? Was it Tom Bailey? He'd been with Webb earlier. Maybe Tom wanted to kill me too. My breath shrieked in my ears, scalded my throat and lungs.

I made out a shadowy form ahead of me. I stopped short and ducked behind a big pine. Could Webb have slipped past me somehow or was this one of the others?

I didn't think I could summon strength for another go round, but I knew I had to. I pressed my body tight against the rough bark. The footsteps came closer. I tried to steady my breathing. I didn't dare peek out around the trunk. I psyched myself to hit and run. I'd done it once. I could do it again, I told myself. A figure came into view. Jim, Jim Thompson.

Had I really found fault with him, accused him of not keeping me in the loop on the investigation? In a matter of seconds, I took back any negative thought I'd ever had about Jim Thompson. I stepped out from behind the tree and, with the last ounce of strength I could muster, I careened toward him

He didn't bellow. He didn't roar. He didn't even ask a question. For once, he was speechless.

I needed a few seconds to catch my breath. Then I said, "Jim, Brian Webb just tried to kill me."

CHAPTER THIRTY-NINE

JIM GOT AN arm around my waist and supported me along the dirt road toward the Beach House. The storm had wreaked havoc across the campground. The ground was littered, not just with broken branches and tree trunks, but with shattered picnic tables, collapsed tents and the twisted remnants of camping equipment. As Jim guided me around these obstacles and out of the woods, I recounted the details of both attacks.

"Those men Tammy Stevenson listed in her notebook. They're involved in some kind of consortium. Not Arthur Brown, I don't think, and there may be others she didn't list, but Phil and some other guys have a big deal in the works."

"How big?" Jim asked. He was almost carrying me now.

"A casino, big enough to kill people over," I said.

"And you came close to being one of those killed, looks like."

As we reached the Beach House lawn, Rick Cronin came running toward us. Jim handed me off to him and took off back into the woods.

Rick helped me up the steps and into the Beach House lobby. Twenty or thirty injured, some of them children, lay on the floor as their families hovered around them. Babies wailed. Medical personnel moved from one victim to another, kneeling to examine them and administer first aid.

"Three or four ambulances have already left with the worst hurt," Rick told me as he eased me into a chair just inside the door.

He signaled one of the rescue workers. "This is our mayor. She's banged up pretty bad. Somebody's got to take a look at her."

"I can wait," I said. The lobby was full of people who needed help more than I did.

"Then let's find you a room where you can have some privacy," Rick said.

"No. No, thank you. I'll just wait right here with everyone else. I'm anxious to find out about the storm damage." No point in telling him I'd be scared to death to be alone right then. In fact, I wouldn't be anxious to stay alone anywhere until I knew Brian Webb had been found and arrested.

Rick filled me in on the storm. "They're saying it was a tornado. We don't get too many up here, but they didn't have to tell me what it was. I saw it coming at us. It raced right through the campgrounds, took down trees, tipped over trailers. Exactly the way they describe a tornado."

I focused enough to remember Jamie and his mother.

"Do you remember seeing a woman come in here with a two-year-old named Jamie," I asked him.

"No. It's been a mob scene here–lost kids, parents going nuts looking for them. A real mess. Ambulances have already taken the worse injured. A couple people looked to be hurt bad. Maybe more still out there. I probably should get back, if you're sure you don't need me to stay with you," he said.

As soon as I'd assured him I was all right, Rick took off to join in the search for more storm victims. Once he was out of sight, I struggled to my feet and over to a big wing chair where I could curl up. The chair's upholstery was already so stained by water and dirt I couldn't make it any worse. After today, Phil would need a lot more than soft lighting to hide his lobby's flaws.

"I'll be over to check you out in a minute, Ms. Graham," one of the EMTs called to me.

"No hurry. I'm okay." I thought I was. I made cautious movements with my arms and legs. Everything hurt like crazy, but not enough to indicate fractures. I leaned back against the soggy chair cushions and let my eyes close. As long as I was in a crowded room, I'd be safe.

I'd fallen into a light sleep when I sensed someone leaning over me. Startled, I bolted up, my heart racing. Phil Johnson brought his face close to mine and spoke in a harsh whisper.

"Loren, are you all right?"

The nerve of the man. "God damn it, Phil. No. I'm not all right. Somebody tried to kill me. You were there. You know that."

He patted my arm, as if quieting a difficult child.

"Take it easy, Loren. I don't think anyone meant to kill you."

Amazing. He was putting his own spin on what had happened. "Damn it, Phil. I'm telling you Brian Webb tried to kill me. You got him away from me once, but he came back and he meant business."

A succession of emotions flitted across his face—surprise, disbelief, then finally, a dawning awareness that I was telling the truth.

"The hell you say. You don't mean it."

"Yes, I do mean it. Brian Webb. He came back to kill me." I began to shake as the memories rushed back—the raised arm wielding the branch, the whoosh of air as the makeshift weapon catapulted toward my head, the blow to my shoulder. "It was just good luck that I got away. He really meant to do it. He said so. He asked me why I didn't die before. Then he said maybe I did."

He glanced around to see if anyone was listening.

"Keep your voice down, Loren. You know I was the one stopped him. You must remember that. I stopped him."

"That first time you did, but I'm telling you he found me again."

He believed me finally. "Oh, God, Loren. I never signed on to do murder. Damn it. I thought Tom had found a way to get that girl to leave town, that Tammy Stevenson. She got money out of me one time, so I knew how she operated. She started working for Tom and the next thing I knew she was gone. He claimed he gave her enough so she'd take off. Then when they found her body…"

"And you never told anybody what you suspected?"

"Tom's got a temper, but he's all bluster. I really didn't think he killed her. Webb either. Then, Deke starts giving trouble, wants them to give back the money he put in. Next thing I know, he's dead. John Roberts and me, we didn't dare cross 'em after that. We could have been next." His voice thickened with fear.

"You guessed right about crossing Webb. He would have killed you easy and it wouldn't have bothered him one bit." I flashed on that demon face above me. The stuff of a hundred nightmares to come.

As I turned away, trying to collect myself, I saw Rick Cronin and Don Morrison crossing the lobby toward us.

Phil pulled Rick aside.

"What the hell's going on with Webb? Have you found him?"

As Rick described the search, Don squatted down next to my chair and put a protective arm around my shoulders.

"Damn it, Loren. I've been trying to make a move on you. Would you please stay alive long enough for me to do it?" he said.

185

I felt as if a gust of fresh air had blown into the room. "You better hurry then. Apparently, I can't give any guarantees."

One of the EMTs shooed the men aside and checked me over.

"I don't just like the look of those head injuries, Ms. Graham. You ought to let an Emergency Room doc check you out."

Don volunteered to take me to the hospital. "I can drive her down there. Be quicker than waiting around for an ambulance. We can leave her car here."

"I'll find somebody to take it down to her house for her. I know the drill," Rick Cronin said.

I tried to object, but the words didn't come out.

Before we could get underway, Jim came striding through the front door and over to us. His posture, his expression, everything about him told me he'd found Brian Webb, but I needed to hear him say the words.

"Remind me not to piss you off any time soon, Mayor. I can't even charge Webb with resisting arrest you did such a job on him," he said.

Relief flooded through me.

"Where did you find him?"

"Right near where you clobbered him. His knee took quite a hit."

"You know what? I don't feel the least bit guilty about it. I think he killed Tammy Stevenson, maybe Deke Dolley, too. And he sure wanted to kill me."

Jim nodded, although I wasn't sure exactly which of my accusations he was agreeing with.

"Next thing I know, you'll be asking for a piece of my salary on this one, Mayor. You may have called it right. Except we're not sure yet about Tom Bailey. He's taken off for parts unknown, we think. If you run into him, better not go out of your way to chat him up."

Before Jim could say more, Don interrupted, "I'd like to run her down to the ER, Jim. Then I think I'd better keep her at my place until you get this thing straightened out."

Jim couldn't agree fast enough. Male bonding, I guess you'd call it. "He's right about that, Mayor. A night or two out of town would be a good move on your part. Give me a chance to get this cleared up. I'll be down to talk with you there in the morning."

Everything was decided without my vote, but I hurt too much to object. Don drove me to the Glens Falls Hospital. The emergency room was jammed with injured from the tornado, but I rated a stretcher in the hall, a checkup by a harried young doctor and a series of tests. Same findings as the EMTs–battered, bruised, nothing broken.

Don picked up some takeout on the way to his house and settled me on the couch in his living room.

"Hope you like Chinese," he said as he opened half a dozen containers and spread them out on the coffee table in front of us. They gave off a heavenly aroma, but as soon as I'd taken the first few bites of seafood war bar, my eyelids drooped shut.

I sank back on the couch, but Don pulled me to my feet and guided me into his bedroom.

"You'll stay in here. I've got air, so the windows can be closed and locked. Here's a towel and my best pair of pajamas. I'm sleeping right outside on the couch. I'll hear you if you need anything."

I offered a weak smile. I wasn't concerned about needing something. I just didn't want anybody dropping by to finish me off. Much as I hated to admit it, having Don on guard duty was better than a sleeping pill.

Chapter Forty

By the time Jim arrived a little after nine the next morning, I was orchestrating my return to life. I limped into the living room and accepted the pain pills and mug of coffee Don handed me. I caught Jim's sideways glance at the blankets and pillow still on the couch.

"We're charging Brian Webb with the murder of Tammy Stevenson, Mayor. Not sure yet of the charges for his attack on you. Attempted murder would be my choice. Don't know if we can get Tom Bailey as an accessory. I've got two or three witnesses say Webb picked Tammy up from Vic's the night she disappeared, but no one claims to have seen Tom with them."

I thought of how Webb had come back after me at the campgrounds. He'd traveled alone then too. Maybe that was the way he operated.

"What's going to happen to the others in the consortium?" I asked him. "Phil Johnson told me he gave Webb money for lobbying. And Peter Finch and Mr. Roberts must have too. That's why they're all so strapped."

"Why don't we all sit down in the kitchen?" Don said. "I've got a fresh pot of coffee and some sweet rolls. Do you both good to eat something."

As we settled ourselves at Don's kitchen table, Jim said, "So far, we haven't turned up any criminal activity to charge them with. They're talking rather freely now. They admit to being in over their heads financially. They borrowed money for Webb to use in the effort to bring a casino here," Jim said.

I nodded. "That was the purpose of their consortium, I guess. But Deke couldn't come up with enough money and Arthur Brown told me he was invited to join, but wouldn't do it."

"Arthur's a smart old bird. The others should have gone along with him," Jim said.

"Do you know yet how Tammy Stevenson fit into all this," I asked.

"Well, as I guess you realize, she started out getting money from men the old-fashioned way--drunken seductions. Then, she apparently stumbled on papers at Tom Bailey's motel outlining plans for casino gambling on the Point and figured she'd hit pay dirt."

"You mean she threatened to tell about the plans for the casino?" I asked.

"That's how I understand it. She'd only asked for five hundred dollars to keep quiet about the sexual encounters, but she really upped the ante when she found out about the casino. Webb wouldn't chance letting her make those plans public."

I shuddered. I tried to block out the image of Tammy's lifeless body on the side of that hill, but I couldn't do it.

"So, was Tom Bailey involved in killing her? He was at the campground with Webb, and I think he was one of the men who talked about killing me. Why wasn't his name in Tammy's little book?"

Jim shook his head. "I can't say for sure yet. With Tom and Webb so thick, if she tried to blackmail Tom about the casino plans, she might have signed her own death warrant the minute she mentioned she'd seen them."

I shuddered. "Do you think Tom was involved in her murder?"

"He could have been. Or, Webb could have done it easy enough without help. Tom's always been friends with the Taggerts. Lately, he's had quite a flirtation going with Melissa. Maybe he's been trying to figure out what they knew about Tammy's blackmail schemes. I'm letting him sweat a little. Want him to turn on Webb."

I brought up something else that was bothering me.

"Jim, about Deke Dolley. I can't shake the feeling there's something more there. Remember that morning when he was shot and Ramona claimed she heard someone in the cabin with him? Then at the hospital, she acted scared to death, wouldn't take her eyes off him, like she expected someone to come after him there."

"Ramona might have suspected someone of killing Deke, but the coroner ruled his death a suicide. He found nothing to indicate foul play," Jim said.

"Did Ramona ever show you the note she found?" I asked him.

"Said it was too personal and she burned it. Claimed Jeannie told her it was okay," Jim said.

"But Jeannie lied about the suicide note," I insisted. "I know it wasn't on the sideboard the morning Deke was shot. I think Jeannie faked the note somehow and gave it to Ramona the next day."

"That's a possibility, of course. But there's no way now we're going to prove Deke didn't write it. Maybe she was just trying to give her mother–what did she call it? Closure?"

"If she was trying to put her mother's mind at rest, I have to admit she succeeded. Ramona was like a different person after she read the note." I recalled how calm Ramona had seemed that Sunday morning at Jeannie's house as she relayed the news of Deke's death.

"I don't think I can tie Webb to Deke's murder," Jim said, "even though he was obviously capable of it. I do have a statement from one of the others implicating him in the break-ins–Tammy's car, your car, your house. And we know he was the one who attacked you both times at the campground. The first time he wanted to find out what was in Tammy's notebook, see how much trouble it was going to make for them."

"But the second time he wanted to kill me. If I hadn't been able to grab that branch..."

"That's enough for now." Don, who'd been sitting quietly listening to our conversation, jumped to his feet. "Better take a break, you two. Let me give you both more coffee and Danish. There must be other things we can talk about."

We tried. We talked about the storm and the damage to the campgrounds and the cost to the town, but I had one more question and I had to ask it.

So I did.

"Jim, have you thought Jeannie Spenser might have been a silent partner in the consortium? She's linked one way or another to all the local people. Jane Finch mentioned dealing with her, Phil Johnson, too, even Mr. Roberts."

As I spoke I remembered Jeannie's whispered conversation with Tom Bailey in her kitchen the morning after Deke's death and the comment Ramona had made, 'Jeannie's got her finger in so many pies around here.'

Jim chose his words with care. "If she was in it, she was clever enough to cover her tracks. There could be evidence somewhere of her involvement, but we may never find it."

"Maybe," I said, "it's like one of those hidden things Matt the douser searches for. Sometimes it's not where you think it is. And sometimes, no matter where you look, you never find it."

"But sometimes," Jim said, "if you're patient, it turns up when you least expect it."

Chapter Forty-one

IN THE AFTERMATH of the September 11th terrorist attacks on New York and Washington, with huge amounts of money sucked out of the state coffers, New York State Governor George Pataki signed into law the largest gambling expansion legislation in the state's history.

Plans called for three casinos in the western part of the state to be run by the Senecas on their own tribal lands and three others-- the off-reservation casinos the consortium was hoping for–to be operated by the St. Regis Mohawk tribe in the Catskills. The consortium might have kept Emerald Point in the competition for a while, but they were no match for the Catskills where promoters spent an estimated two million dollars in their efforts to locate the off-reservation casinos there.

I won't deny I had moments when I wished we were looking at that kind of prosperity for Emerald Point, without the problems I knew would come with it, of course. But I was too busy with our immediate concerns to think about might-have-beens.

The tornado had done thousands of dollars worth of damage in our area. We qualified for some disaster relief; our bank agreed to loans; a financial adviser volunteered his expertise; we even arranged a few tax breaks for our hard-hit businesses.

Help was available, but the research and the tallying of losses took an incredible amount of time. When Don Morrison discovered how backed up we were, he pitched in and applied his considerable skills to filing the applications.

All that fall, Emerald Point's mood, like the rest of the country's, was somber. The consortium members struggled for ways to survive the winter. Ramona rented a couple of rooms in her house. Jack Roberts left his father to deal with the Inn's problems on his own and took a job managing a Ramada downstate. Phil Johnson offered a leaf peeking special and recouped enough to start minor renovations. Peter and Jane Finch sold their motel at a loss and moved away. Tom Bailey, after narrowly escaping charges, let Jeannie Spenser find him a buyer for his motel.

One cool fall night after a particularly tough week, I'd agreed to meet for a pizza at Mario's. I'd just parked my car when I saw Jeannie Spenser emerge from the front door, loaded down with takeout containers.

"Jeannie, what are you doing up here?" I walked over to her.

"Taking dinner to my mother's. She doesn't feel like going out yet," she said.

Patience be damned, I had to find out what she knew.

"What have you heard about Tom Bailey's case? Is he going to get out of this or not?" I asked her.

"He's got a good attorney. He'll probably be all right, but it'll cost him. He'll need most of the money he realizes from the sale of his motel to pay his legal bills."

"That still beats going to jail. And if he was involved in Tammy Stevenson's murder..." I watched her face, trying to gauge her reaction.

"I don't think Tom was guilty of anything but stupidity. Those guys were so foolish. You shouldn't play a game if you don't have the brains or guts for it. I tried to tell them that, but all they could see were dollar signs."

What was she telling me?

"Jeannie, you assured me once better things were on the horizon for Emerald Point. I thought you agreed with what they were doing."

She set her bags down on the sidewalk next to her.

"Loren, give me credit. Their scheme was a big gamble. I thought at first it might be worth a look-see. Then I put out some feelers to people I know in the Catskills. Emerald Point was competing with big names down there. I tried to convince these guys they were out of their league, but they wouldn't listen."

"You tried to dissuade them?"

"I talked to each of them separately. Not Deke, of course. He was out almost before he was in. That man couldn't do anything right, even commit suicide."

The coldness in her voice shocked me.

"Did he, Jeannie? Commit suicide, I mean? Or did someone kill him?"

"Kill him? Why would you think somebody killed him? My mother was afraid to admit it was suicide because of the insurance."

Her surprise seemed genuine.

"But that suicide note. I know it wasn't on the sideboard the day he was shot. I looked there."

I thought I'd gone too far, but she didn't hesitate.

"Of course, it wasn't. I wrote that note. You probably think that's terrible, but my mother was a wreck. She knew Deke was involved in something, thought someone had wanted to kill him, maybe wanted to kill her, too. That note changed everything. You saw how different she was after I gave it to her."

She was answering my questions, so I asked the one I most wanted her to answer.

"Jeannie, are you saying you didn't have money in that scheme yourself?"

Her startled expression told me I'd made an incredible gaffe.

"Loren, give me a break. I didn't build my business by taking foolish risks. Before I make an investment, I examine the pros and cons. I don't get on board until I'm sure the train is going to leave the station. That scheme was full of holes. Look, my food's getting cold. I've got to go." She snatched up her bags and walked away.

I turned and went inside Mario's.

I mulled over what she said as I waited for Don. Jeannie might pepper her talk with clichés, but I had the feeling she'd told me the truth. Maybe she was only offering me closure, as she'd done with her mother, but I believed her. The consortium members probably did invite Jeannie to join, just as they'd invited Arthur Brown. Bottom line—the smart people had been smart enough to say 'no.'

When Don arrived a few minutes later, I didn't tell him about my conversation with Jeannie. I wanted to keep it to myself until I had a chance to think it through. But for the first time since I'd found Tammy Stevenson's body, I felt a sense of relief as if the last loose end had been tied up.

Don and I talked of other things as we ate our pizza—the usual half sausage for him, half mushroom for me.

After our waitress had wrapped the leftovers for Don, I made a suggestion.

"You know, you keep telling me how great pizza tastes for breakfast and I've never tried it. Maybe I should come home with you and find out for myself."

Don stared at me for thirty seconds, then signaled for our check.

And you know what? He was right.

Anne White's first Lake George Mystery, **An Affinity For Murder**, was awarded a Malice Domestic Unpublished Writers' Grant in 1999, chosen a winner in the Oak Tree Press Dark Oak Contest in 2000 and received a Malice Domestic Best First Mystery nomination in 2002. **Beneath The Surface,** introduces Loren Graham, a former New Yorker, who's adopted the Lake George area as her home.

White is a member of Mystery Writers of America, Sisters in Crime, the Lake George Arts Project and the Unusual Suspects, a Saratoga Springs writers group. She is married and the mother of six children.